"What are you doing?" I asked, when Chelsie picked up the phone.

"Emoting," she said. "That's kind of like acting, but with lots more emotion. Emoting, emotion. Get it?"

"I get it. Why are you emoting?"

"Mr. Snow just announced auditions for *Romeo and Juliet,* the play Keats is putting on in May." Her voice turned disgusted. "Everyone in the whole school wanted to do *Brigadoon* except these two snobby ninth graders. They railroaded it through. Anyway, I'm practicing. I made up this alphabetical list of emotions, and I'm going to practice every single one. Indignation. That's next."

"Well, good luck," I said, getting this funny twinge. *I* wanted to be in that show! Maybe even play Juliet, depending on who was Romeo. Victoria Mahoney, star. Maybe if I practiced emoting. . . .

# TAKE A BOW, VICTORIA

Shelly Nielsen

**Chariot Books**
DAVID C. COOK PUBLISHING CO.

A White Horse Book
Published by Chariot Books,
an imprint of David C. Cook Publishing Co.
David C. Cook Publishing Co., Elgin, Illinois
David C. Cook Publishing Co., Weston, Ontario

TAKE A BOW, VICTORIA
© 1986 by Shelly Nielsen

Cover illustration by Gail Roth
Design by Barbara Sheperd Tillman

Printed in the United States of America
90 89          5 4 3

Library of Congress Cataloging-in-Publication Data
Nielsen, Shelly, 1958-
    Take a bow, Victoria.
    (A White horse book)
    Summary: Besides the embarrassment of her pregnant
mother's coming to school and her grandmother's working on
a school production, Victoria must deal with her own mixed
desires of being a star or remaining safely backstage.
    [1. Schools—Fiction. 2. Family life—Fiction]
I. Title.
PZ7.N5682Tak 1986          [Fic]          86-8818
ISBN 0-89191-470-6

*for some snazzy grandparents—*
*Alma, Orva, and Henry*

# 1

"Chelsie, is that you?"

The girl in the flouncy, old-fashioned dress turned and grinned at me with bright red lips. "Of course it's me. Don't you recognize your own best friend?"

Chelsie Bixler and I have been friends since we were little, and we have lockers right next to each other in the seventh-grade hall at Keats Junior High School. But even I could barely recognize her in that getup.

"Do I look like a star?"

"You look different," I said. "Can I have your autograph?"

She posed by the door marked "Stage" and

twirled around for me to get a good look. She had a big part in the school play, *Oklahoma!*, tonight. Her dark hair was all done up. She had the pinkest cheeks you ever saw. And eye shadow. Blue eye shadow about an inch thick.

"What are you doing back here, anyway?" she asked. "The show's going to start any second."

"I have a message from your fan club."

"What fan club?"

"Your parents, my parents, and my dumb little brother. They told me to tell you to 'break a leg.' That's stage talk for good luck."

"I know, I know. I'm an actress. Don't you think I know the lingo?"

I started to explain where our seats were in the auditorium in case she wanted to give us a secret sign or a wink or something, but she wasn't listening. She was holding up a compact and putting more lipstick on. Her mouth was already enormous.

I poked her. "Your padding is slipping."

"Whoops, you're kidding. Thanks, Vic. That could have been a disaster."

"What's this thing sticking out over here?"

"A bustle. Don't you know anything about old-time fashion? Women used to wear bustles and bonnets and stuff."

"Looks uncomfortable."

"It is. And hot. I'm sweating like crazy. Feel."

Her hands were really sweaty, all right.

8

"I better go," I said. "I want to get back to my seat before they turn down the lights. Good luck. I'll be the one clapping loudest."

Chelsie went through the stage door and I went back into the noisy auditorium. I was nervous. And I wasn't even in the show.

"Did you see her?" Dad asked, after I crawled over the Bixlers to reach my seat.

I was about to tell him about her crazy makeup and sweaty hands when the French horn player in the junior high orchestra started blasting out notes. She must have been showing off for someone, because the orchestra leader suddenly threw down his baton. It looked as though he were aiming at her.

"Have you ever seen a bustle, Dad? She had on a bustle."

"I know what a bustle is, but they weren't exactly common fashion accessories during my lifetime. I wasn't born during the Civil War, you know."

The audience was snickering. Someone was poking his head out between the stained, gold velvet curtains.

"When's it gonna start?" said Matthew in his whiney, five-year-old voice.

I twisted around to see if the doors were being shut yet. That's a sign that the show's going to start. That's when I saw Mom was coming.

There was no mistaking Mom, even though the lights were low. She was the only woman there

9

with a gigantic, pregnant stomach. Down the aisle she walked in her ugly maternity top. Waddled was more like it.

"Over here, Mom!" Matthew called, standing on his seat and waving before Dad could yank him back down.

The crowd laughed. I slid down in my seat so that no one would recognize the back of my head.

"I'm more entertaining than any old musical," said Mom cheerfully, squishing into the seat next to Dad.

"They're jealous," gushed Dad. "You're one vibrant, expectant mother."

*Maybe I'll die right here,* I thought, *maybe I'll die of shame right in the middle of the Keats Junior High School auditorium.*

Luckily, the orchestra leader rapped for attention then, and the lights dimmed. The orchestra crashed into the overture to *Oklahoma!*

Before Chelsie even came out, I noticed two big problems with the play. Number one, the main character's name is Curly because he has curly hair. Bryant Borwanski, who was playing Curly, had straight hair. At least they could have curled his hair for the show. The other thing was that the orchestra wasn't so hot. The trumpets couldn't hit the notes. Every once in a while they'd make a high note, but then they would slide back down. Ooo. I cringed in my seat.

Mr. and Mrs. Bixler were grinning their heads

off, I noticed. My parents, too. Parents are like that. They don't get embarrassed about anything.

Chelsie didn't come out until after a couple of songs. By that time I was sweating like crazy. That's the trouble with having friends in drama. You've got to go to all their performances and be nervous for them.

She was pretty good! I sat up straighter. Chelsie is not the world's best singer, but she really belted out her number.

The only terrible thing that happened was during the song about "poor Jud is dead." A cardboard windmill near the edge of the stage started to sway. Curly just kept right on singing, of course: "Poor Jud is dead, poor Jud Fry is dead."

When he got to the second "dead," the windmill finally toppled over and fell. The guy playing Jud got it right in the head. I'll bet his poor old skull ached.

In the end, Laurie marries Curly, Ado Annie gets together with Will, Oklahoma becomes a state, and everyone lives happily ever after. Not exactly realistic stuff, but fun.

I clapped my head off. When the actors came running out during the curtain call, Mom jumped up to give them a standing ovation, which was sort of humiliating. Why couldn't she just be small and unnoticeable like other mothers? But then Mr. and Mrs. Bixler stood up, too, and then Matthew. I looked around, and everyone in the audience was standing up. I jumped up and clapped as hard as I could.

Backstage I had to wedge between a bunch of people to be the first one to shake Chelsie's hand. She was still wearing her bustly dress, and her makeup was a little smeared.

"You were great!" I shrieked, grabbing her slightly sweaty hands and jumping around.

"You're just saying that," she said. "I can't sing to save my life." But she sounded happy.

"It was perfect. I mean, Ado Annie's kind of a dip, right? So she's not supposed to be a great singer. I think you did it perfectly."

Then she really looked happy. "Yeah, you're probably right."

"There she is, the star!" It was my mom, sticking out her arms and running to give Chelsie a hug. I could tell Chelsie's never been hugged by an eight-month-pregnant woman before; there's this problem about where you put her stomach.

Mrs. Bixler was next. She put her arm around Chelsie's shoulders and squeezed a little, but carefully, so she wouldn't get any of Chelsie's makeup on her white sweater. She looked very proud and happy.

Mr. Bixler called her "Pumpkin" (Chelsie's face went red under all the makeup), and Dad shook her hand and told her she was the next stage great. Matthew didn't want to congratulate Chelsie at all. He wanted to stand on the stage. He even went up and blew into a microphone to see if it was working. Sometimes he can really be a brat.

"Everyone's invited to our house for dessert!" Mr. Bixler announced, laughing. Mr. Bixler always laughs when he talks. I bet he'd make a great Santa Claus. Ho, ho, ho.

# 2

"I wish I could act."

That's what I said under my breath on the way home from the Bixlers' house later that night. Mom was singing this loud, corny song from the play called "People Will Say We're in Love," and I didn't think anyone would hear me. But suddenly everyone in the car got quiet and looked at me.

"You can act," said Mom. "I've seen you. Remember the time I wanted you to try on that cute little dress at Penney's? You had a fit."

"That was no act. Do you have any idea what would have happened to me if I'd shown up at school in a dress with bows on it, for Pete's sake?" I groaned, just thinking about it.

"What makes you think you can't act?" Dad said. "Have you ever tried?"

"Don't need to. I'd be too petrified to open my mouth, practically."

"I know what you mean. I get stage fright, too. Which is why I became a chef. Cooks can talk to cabbages and pie dough all day instead of people."

"You talk to cabbages, Dad?" Matthew asked, breaking up.

"Well," said Dad, "just on slow days."

"Since when are you interested in acting?" Mom asked, twisting around to look at me. "I thought you wanted to be a writer."

"Isn't there such a thing as a part-time actor?" I asked. Acting, even part-time acting, seemed glamorous. Everyone crowded around and told you that you looked ravishing. Little kids came up and asked for your autograph. Your parents threw parties for you, complete with homemade ice cream.

"Romeo, Romeo, where fort art you, Romeo?" said Matthew dramatically, throwing out his arms in the backseat and practically chopping me in the neck.

"With all the theaters around town, we should go to more plays," Mom was saying.

Great. I could just imagine my mom and her big stomach in the Guthrie—this world-famous theater in Minneapolis—coming down the aisle and making the whole highbrow audience snicker. Even the idea humiliated me.

15

Mom snapped her fingers. "Hey, I have a great idea. There's another production coming up at the end of the year, isn't there? If you don't want to suffer stage fright, you could take a production job."

"What's that?" I asked suspiciously.

"You know—lighting, sets, costumes. You don't have to act to be involved in a show."

*Unless you want any of the glamour,* I thought. But I didn't say it aloud.

"Yeah," said Dad. "Hasn't your mother ever told you about her days as a lighting supervisor in college? She invited me to the opening night of *The Taming of the Shrew* and—"

"Terry," said my mother in a warning voice. "Don't you dare tell that story."

"—and right in the middle of Act II, there was this tremendous commotion overhead."

"Just a little noise."

"A little noise? It was a racket! So we all looked up and there were two legs—attached to your mother, of course—dangling from the rafters."

"I slipped," said Mom sheepishly. "I was up there making some final adjustments, and I lost my footing."

"Then what happened?" asked Matthew, all ears.

"I pulled myself back up, of course. The cast was furious with me for wrecking the show. Anyway, what I started to say is that there are a lot of exciting jobs you can do on a play besides act."

Somehow Vickie Mahoney, lighting supervisor, didn't sound as glamorous as Victoria Hope Mahoney, star.

"Maybe," said Dad, "you should just forget about being an actor, forget about being a writer, and become a chef—like your old man."

"Ugh!" Matthew groaned. "Vickie can't even cook toast."

"I CAN, TOO!"

Mom interrupted, or we would have had a great fight. "Prove it, tomorrow. I have a late doctor's appointment, and I won't be home till after dinner. You can make the meal."

"You're not leaving me alone with these two hoodlums again, are you, Bob?" my father asked in a horrified voice.

"They're not so bad. You get used to them after an hour or so."

*Another* doctor's appointment.

"I'm sure going to be glad when this baby is born," I said. "It takes all of your time." My voice surprised me. It had a hot edge of anger to it.

Mom gave a laugh. "Don't tell me you think the baby will be less work after he—or she—is born! Don't you remember how much time Matthew took?"

I remembered. "Oh, yeah."

"Not that you weren't worth it all, honey," said

17

Mom, giving him a pat over the car seat.

Dad twisted the steering wheel, and we pulled into our driveway. "Get the door?" he asked.

I climbed out to heave up the squeaky garage door and beat Matthew to the front door. Bullrush was waiting, twitching his tail and meowing sawed-off meows of welcome. The house felt warm and welcoming. Good old house. Dad was third to the door, with Mom a slow and awkward fourth.

"Head up to bed, okay?" said Dad. "It's late."

During my prayers, Mom tiptoed upstairs. At least she was trying to tiptoe. She sounded like a herd of pregnant zebras. My door creaked open.

"Sorry," she whispered. "Didn't mean to inter-rupt your prayers." She moved Bullrush out of the way and sat on my bed until I was finished.

When I got to the amen, she added softly: "And thanks for a fabulous daughter, Vickie."

We opened our eyes.

"I just came up to say good night," she told me, stroking the blankets smooth around me.

She looked puffy in the lamplight. Normally my Mom is very thin. She looked swollen.

"One thing I forgot to ask you, Mom. I promised Chels I'd help with her lines after school tomorrow. Can Matthew go to the neighbors?"

"Sure. I'll tell him to go straight to the Johnstons'."

We have these great neighbors who don't mind Matthew just dropping in on them any old time. I don't know how they stand it.

She said good night, sleep tight, and crept back downstairs. I got back down on my knees. I asked God to forgive me for being embarrassed about her that night at school. For the most part, she's a pretty good mom.

# 3

When I got to school the next morning, a group of girls I sort of knew were clustered in a circle near my locker. *Ignore them*, I thought.

I have this one particular fear. I'm afraid that someday I'll say, "Hi, everyone!" and everyone will just ignore me. It's humiliating to be ignored. Probably Freud would have loved to analyze me.

Quietly, I opened my locker. No one even noticed. One girl was talking real loudly:

"—and then he said, 'Chelsie, you're gonna miss your cue.' And I said—"

Suddenly I realized that it was Chelsie, telling one of her stories. She had everyone wrapped around her little finger.

"Did you really have to kiss Charles Wingdahl?" Peggy Hiltshire asked, laying on her Mississippi accent.

"Not exactly. We kind of kissed cheeks."

"It looked really real."

"Hi, Vic!" yelled Chels, noticing me.

Then everyone turned around and said hi. Relief.

"We were talking about *Oklahoma!*" said Lynette. "How does it feel to be best friends with the star of the show? Want to be treasurer of the Chelsie Bixler Fan Club?"

Chels giggled. I could tell she liked all the attention.

"I'll be treasurer," I said, "but I won't sign her name on all those publicity photos. No way."

Everyone laughed and spread out to include me in the circle. It's a nice feeling, being included.

"Were you at the play last night, Vickie?" someone asked.

"Of course she was at the play," said Chels. "Where else would a bosom buddy be on opening night?"

"How could you miss her, anyway?" asked Peggy. "That was her mother—you know—" She made a motion like a big stomach in front of her.

"Oh, I remember now," said Lynette, and everyone laughed. Probably I was blushing red. Make that purple.

Then Charita wanted to borrow my science notes, and Chels wanted to walk with me to our humanities class, and I stopped feeling weird. But I was still a little embarrassed. It was taking Mom forever to have that baby.

It was a long day. On the way home, all Chelsie would talk about was the play. She talked about how she almost forgot her lines once, and how Bryant Borwanski was so funny, and how she had three more performances to get through.

"You're still coming over, aren't you?" she asked when we got to our house gate.

It was too late to back out now; I had promised. Besides, maybe it would be good practice for me, just in case I made the play in May.

"I already asked," I said. "Let's go."

We walked on to Chelsie's.

I only got silly once, during the love scene. I couldn't be serious. I think Chels was a little bugged, but it was fun anyway. At 5:30 I said I had to go. She walked me to the front door.

"I'll call you after the show tonight," she said, "if it doesn't get too late."

I ran all the way home. I was a little late and I wanted to beat Dad home.

Inside, the house smelled unusual.

I shut the front door slowly, trying to figure it out. Usually when I get home from school the house doesn't smell like food, because Mom doesn't get home until after five-thirty or so, so there's never anything cooking. So what was that smell? It was definitely food. *Don't tell me Matthew's cook-*

22

*ing*, I thought. I dropped my books and ran into the kitchen.

"Oh," I said. "Mrs. Johnston!"

Our next-door neighbor turned from the stove. She was stirring something in a saucepan, and suddenly I recognized the smell. Macaroni and cheese. And wieners. Wieners under the broiler. I hate wieners.

Matthew was sitting quietly at the table. He looked at me with a lost-puppy expression. He didn't know what was going on, either.

"I hope I didn't startle you," she said. "I wanted to meet you at the door, but it was getting late and I thought I'd better get dinner started."

A baby-sitter! My parents had gotten Mrs. Johnston to baby-sit! Normally Matthew just goes next door, and she looks after him. What was she doing over here?

"Here, Vickie, you sit down with your brother and eat. Do you want milk? I'll pour you some."

This was strange, very strange. I gave Matthew a look, and he shrugged.

"What's up, Mrs. Johnston? You don't have to cook for us. Actually, I'm a pretty good cook."

"She is not," said Matthew, and I almost slugged him.

Mrs. Johnston acted as though she didn't even hear me. She was spooning great orange globs of cheesy macaroni onto our plates, right from the pan. *When she brings that hot dog over here and puts it in front of me,* I thought, *I'll die. I'll actually die.*

"Is Mom going to be home soon?" I asked, trying not to breathe the fumes. "How late is her appointment?"

Mrs. Johnston bit down on her lip. "I—I don't know. I mean, after you eat I'm going to drive you over to the hospital. Your father will explain everything."

"She's having the baby early!" I yelled, excited.

Mrs. Johnston's face was a cross between angry and scared. "Your father will tell you everything," she said again.

Matthew and I ate slowly, like it was a normal meal, while Mrs. Johnston washed dishes and put leftover macaroni in a plastic container. The silence made me a nervous wreck.

Something was very, very wrong, I decided during the long ride to the hospital. Something was wrong with Mom. But I didn't have any more questions to ask Mrs. Johnston. I was too scared.

Dad was waiting for us behind the big sliding glass doors at the hospital. He came toward us slowly.

"Thanks, Millie," he said. "You've been a big help."

"Is everything—?" she asked, her eyebrows up.

"No change. I'll call you."

Mrs. Johnston's shoes made a clip-clopping noise on the linoleum as she headed back outside.

"Dad, what's wrong? What's wrong with Mom?"

He made us sit down in the ugly plastic lobby chairs.

"At the clinic today, the doctor couldn't find the baby's heartbeat. Sometime after Mom's last appointment, the baby . . . died. They're going to deliver it now. Mom's okay."

"Maybe it's a mistake, Dad." I couldn't believe he hadn't thought of this already. "The baby probably rolled over and the doctor just couldn't hear the heartbeat."

"No." He shook his head and looked at the floor. "No, it's not a mistake."

The bright lights and the Lysol smell in the lobby started to get to me. *I'm going to throw up*, I thought. *Wieners and macaroni and cheese.*

"I want to talk to Mom," said Matthew. "I want to see how she is."

"Sorry, you guys, you're not allowed. If you were both fourteen you could come upstairs to the maternity ward. But I'll take Mom a message, if you want."

I tried to think of something to tell her. My mind was as white and blank as paper from a new notebook.

"Tell her we're down here," I said. Boy, that was dumb. There was only one other thing I could think of: "Tell her I'll pray."

"Tell her not to be scared," said Matthew. "When I was in the hospital that time, I was really scared. Tell her there's nothing to be scared of."

"Okay. I'm going back upstairs. Sit right over here and watch TV. The receptionist said she'd keep an eye on you. If you feel like going home when I come back, I'll drive you."

Dad was gone for a long time. The operators kept paging Dr. Hazelman on the intercom. Matthew watched TV, and I read magazines that were probably a hundred years old. Dad came down once, but I said we were staying, and I gave Matthew a look that said, "Quiet."

*I bet the doctors were wrong,* I thought after Dad went back upstairs. I had heard about stuff like that. Sometimes they didn't even know when a lady was about to have twins. Doctors made mistakes all the time. Any minute now, a nurse would come rushing out and announce, "It was all a mistake! The baby's fine! Come on up and see your mother!" Then I could say, "I knew it all along! I told you everything would be okay."

About halfway through the evening news I fell asleep. I was dreaming that I was in the chorus of *Oklahoma!* My costume was great, all swirly fabric around my legs, and I was really giving my all to the songs. At the end of the show, the audience gave us a standing ovation. The company all joined hands and bowed. I was so happy, my cheeks hurt from grinning and grinning and grinning.

I woke up. Dad was leaning over the chair, squeezing my shoulder. I sat up. My neck had a kink in it, and my mouth was dry.

"Hi, Dad," I said.

"Hi."

We just looked at each other for a minute. His eyes were bloodshot, and his mouth was a tight, unsmiling line. He had Matthew's hand in his, and he squeezed mine, too, until it hurt.

"Mom's okay," he said. "She's asleep now."

Then I knew it wasn't a mistake.

Our baby was really dead.

# 4

"Victoria, dear, I haven't seen you in ages. Come in, come in."

Mrs. Bixler acted like we were long-lost buddies or something. It had only been a week since I had seen her last, but it seemed like a year to me, too.

She led the way into the house, moving gracefully ahead of Chels and me. At the end of the dark hallway, she hung a left into the kitchen. The room was bright and cheerful and smelled like brownies.

Chels leaned over the counter and switched on the kitchen TV. "Have you ever seen this program? It's really funny. Want to watch the end?"

I pulled up a stool and tried to get interested in the show. Then I noticed Mrs. Bixler staring at me.

28

I looked up, and she smiled sympathetically. "Would you like a brownie, dear?"

"Sure. Yes, please."

If Mrs. Bixler called me "dear" again, I'd scream. Something felt creepy, really creepy. I looked around. Partly it was creepy because Mrs. Bixler was so cheerful, and the kitchen smelled so good, and everything seemed so normal. I shivered.

"How have you been, Vickie?" Mrs. Bixler put a thick slab of brownie on a napkin and set it in front of me.

"Okay, except for my math class. I don't really get along with Mrs. Hartford, but that's nothing new. Other than that, I guess everything's fine."

She nodded, and I bit into my brownie. It was delicious—one of those very chewy kinds.

"And," said Mrs. Bixler, "how's everything—" she paused. "—at home?"

Then I understood what she was getting at. The brownie turned into a lump; I swallowed hard.

"Everything's all right," I said. But that wasn't exactly true. "Actually," I added, "things aren't so hot. Matthew's okay, but Mom and Dad—"

Mrs. Bixler's face went red, and she started brushing brownie crumbs off the counter into her hand. I could tell she didn't want the gory details.

Actually it had been the worst week I could ever remember. Mom was back from the hospital, but she didn't look like herself. She looked as though she'd been stung by a giant bee. Mostly she slept.

And Dad had circles under his eyes, the color of overbaked pie dough. At night I heard them crying together. It's terrible hearing your parents cry. Nothing makes you feel better after that—not writing a poem, not praying, not even petting your cat.

Luckily, Chels rescued me about then. She switched off the TV and spread her arms wide.

"Notice anything different about me?" she asked.

I stared at her and couldn't think of what it was. My mind was hazy, like I'd just woken up.

"I'll give you a hint." She shook her head, and her dark hair brushed her chin.

Suddenly I knew. "You cut your hair!"

"I can't believe it took you all day to notice! I had to wait till after the play to cut it, but then it was chop-chop time. Don't you like it? I told you I wanted a more sophisticated cut."

I took another bite of brownie and chewed on it slowly. I missed her old hairstyle. Why'd she have to cut it? Why did everything have to change?

"It looks good on you," I said.

Mrs. Bixler gave me another brownie without even asking. "Before I forget, dear," she said, "will you ask your parents about dinner? I've been meaning to ask them over. See if they're available next Friday night. I don't want them to bring a thing—just come and enjoy themselves."

"Let's go up to my room," Chels said.

I followed behind her, still stunned about the

30

haircut. You have to understand something about best friends like Chels and me. We always do things together. Even when she buys new earrings or something dumb like that she usually asks me what I think. When you've always done everything together, a new haircut comes as a real shock. Haircuts are much more important than earrings.

"I would have asked you about the haircut, but you seemed kind of . . . depressed." Chels closed the door to her bedroom and flopped backwards onto the bed.

"When did you decide to do it?" I flipped through a stack of envelopes on the dresser. They were all from me.

"I've been thinking about it a long time. I was waiting for the right timing. All of a sudden—" she snapped her fingers—"I just knew."

"Oh." I put down the letters and leaned against the wall, arms crossed. "Well, it's not too short, I guess. You got lucky. The person who cut my hair was really scissor happy. I got scalped."

She sighed. "You told me. About a hundred times."

"Well, it was terrible!" Without warning, I was furiously angry.

"Okay, okay. Vic, loosen up! What's wrong with you? You're so jumpy."

"It hasn't been the greatest week of my life."

She sat up. "Are you okay now?" Her voice had gotten a lot softer.

I shrugged. I almost blabbed everything, how gross everything was at home. I had even been hoping she would invite me to stay over tonight. This morning I'd packed my toothbrush (wrapped in Saran Wrap) in my purse, just in case.

Instead, I sighed. "It's just too complicated to explain."

"I thought we were best friends." Under the sleek haircut, her face formed into a scowl.

"Look, I'm allowed to be depressed every once in a while, aren't I?"

"Vic, you are *exceptionally* jumpy."

Exceptionally? Where'd she pick up a word like exceptionally? Leave it to Chels to start using a phony word like that. She probably got it from all those stuck-up drama club members at Keats.

"I am jumpy," I said, letting my voice get a little too loud. "I'm very jumpy. It's not easy to go through a stillbirth."

That was the new word I'd learned this week; it was what the doctors called Jessica, our baby. It sounded like a peaceful word, but it really felt like bright hospital lights and it smelled like Lysol. It was a word that made me sick to my stomach.

"I know it's not easy to go through stuff like that!" Chelsie yelled back.

I stared at that stupid brownie still crunched in my hand. I wanted to smash it into chocolate syrup.

"Listen," she said, quieter again. "I asked my science teacher, Mr. Freeman, about it. He said an

32

eight-month-old baby isn't really a baby. It's a fetus."

"So what? And what does Mr. Freeman know about it, anyway? To us, she was Jessica, and she was already part of the family!"

Chelsie looked surprised. I was, too, in a way. I didn't know if I actually felt that way about Jessica, or if I was just saying that because my parents did. I stared at the fringe on the bedspread, watching it jiggle when Chels kicked her feet against the bed.

"I was trying to help, but I'm just making things worse. As usual."

I had blown everything up. To cover, I plopped down on the bed, too. Boy. I was turning into a total grouch.

"It's okay," I said.

"No, it's not."

"Yeah, it is."

"No, it's not."

Then we both smiled. There was some brownie in Chelsie's braces.

"Okay, you win," we said at once.

There was a knock. We both jumped about six miles.

"Anyone for more brownies?" called Mrs. Bixler, sticking her head around the door. She had the whole pan with her.

"No, thank you," I said, hoping she didn't notice that I hadn't eaten the last one. It was a mess by now, mashed in the napkin.

33

"Well, anything you do want, just let me know."
She closed the door.

"My mother." Chels rolled her eyes. "She'll probably be like this for a while, because she feels terrible about your mom. I think she has actually wondered if the dessert she fed us the night before caused the whole thing."

"You should tell her it had something to do with the baby's cord. It wasn't the ice cream."

"I can't tell her that!" said Chels. "Cords and birth and babies. My parents are not real big on stuff like that."

She dug around in her dresser. "Want to see some pictures Mr. Snow took of the cast?"

We went through them, one by one.

"I don't suppose things are all that great at your house right now," she said.

"Not so great."

"Guess what? I've been praying for your mom and dad." Her eyes were bright and proud. "I'm taking your advice, Vic. Isn't that great?"

"Thanks," I muttered.

"I've been reading the Bible, too, like you told me to, and I like it. There's some great stuff in there. Jesus seems pretty unusual. He loved everyone. Do you think he still loves everyone, even now? That's what Christians say. Do you think Jesus loves me?"

Then a terrible thing happened. "I don't know," I said, shrugging. It just slipped out.

34

What I meant to say was, "He probably loves you, Chels, but I'm not so sure how he feels about my family, or why would he let this happen? He must know it's practically killing my parents. How could God let that happen? He doesn't love the Mahoneys much at all."

But what I said was, "I don't know."

Chels looked stunned. She muttered something like, "Well, my parents don't believe in Jesus, of course," and then we started talking about this guy at school and that was about all until Chels finally got the hint and invited me to stay over.

I made a quick call home. Mom said, "All right, Vickie, see you tomorrow." She said it in that new, tired voice of hers.

I hung up the phone.

# 5

Of course Mrs. Bixler offered to drive me home
the next morning, but I said no thanks. After the
big breakfast she and Mr. Bixler fixed, I needed the
exercise. I walked myself home.

Spring was finally coming to Minnesota. The
smell of fresh mud was in the air. The sun was
putting out real light. It warmed my face. It made
me feel so good that I said thank you to God in my
mind. I hadn't had anything to thank him for in a
whole week.

Chelsie had cheered me up a little, too. The
great thing about Chels is that she always has a new
plan when things are at their worst. This time it was
a plan for cheering up Mom and Dad, and I

couldn't wait to get home and try it out. Subtly, of course.

"I'm home!" I yelled when I walked in the door.

"Please, Victoria! Could you keep it down?" came my mom's irritable voice.

I couldn't believe it. Mom always says that noise is important. She thinks people should get to make a certain amount of noise. I tiptoed into the family room. Mom was moving a dustcloth around on the furniture. Her eyes were red.

"Did you lock the door?" she asked. As if I were Matthew. As if I were dumb.

"Yeah, I locked it."

I started following her around. When she dusted the coffee table I lifted knickknacks for her to dust under. The timing has to be right. You have to wait until the last second before her cloth hits the spot. Then you lift the knickknack. The last time I did this, she thought it was hysterical. We laughed until we cried, no lie. Today she didn't think it was hysterical. Today she just kept dusting.

"Did you and Chelsie stay up all night again?" she asked.

"Not all night, exactly."

I blabbed all of yesterday's news: how there was a good chance I'd make the all-school spelling bee semifinals, how I had gotten an A- on a pop science quiz. I even told her that Chelsie was driving me nuts talking about being the star of *Oklahoma!*

The whole time I was talking, Mom just nodded.

Once in a while she'd smile, but it was a pretend smile, the kind you use when you've gotten tired of smiling and you're just putting on to be polite. Lately, Mom and Dad had been very polite.

It was definitely time for Chelsie's plan.

"How's your day been, Mom?" I asked, subtly.

"I tried to take a nap and the UPS deliveryman woke me up. Then I started to refinish some woodwork, but I was too tired. So I ended up reading a book that I wasn't interested in." She sighed. "Matthew's at the Johnstons'. Dad, as usual, is at work. I have to get back to Willowood before I go crazy."

Mom is a counselor at a senior citizens' residence called Willowood. She talks to people and helps them feel better about problems and stuff. But how do you make people feel better if *you* feel lousy?

We dusted some more.

"I think I know what would make you feel better, Mom."

"You do?" She stopped suddenly, like she was too tired to go on, and leaned against the TV. She still looked as though she was going to have a baby. The only clothes that fit her were maternity clothes.

"Maybe we should all do something special," I said. "Maybe we should all go out for dessert."

"Dessert? Vickie, somehow I don't think going out for dessert is going to change much."

Chelsie had predicted this. ("They'll say it won't

38

work. Depressed people always say that. Don't let them talk you out of it.")

I started talking fast. "You know that crazy German restaurant by the mall? They sell whole dinners and stuff, but for dessert you can order apple strudel. I bet some apple strudel would cheer us up."

She didn't look convinced. I kept talking. I told her she hadn't lived till she'd tried their apple strudel. I told her I'd treat, with my horde of saved baby-sitting money. I talked myself silly until finally I got her to smile.

"You're persuasive, all right. Okay. After dinner, dessert. The four of us."

Dad drove to the restaurant. It was raining, and no one was saying much except Matthew, who had a new girl friend named Heidi Little. He kept telling us that Heidi said this and Heidi said that. Boy. If I said I had a boyfriend, the whole family would probably flip out. I don't know how he got away with it.

The waitress seated us at a table by the window, so we had a good view of the cars sloshing by with their headlights on. A couple who scuffed by the window threw wet handfuls of leaves at each other.

"Hey," said Matthew, after a bite of strudel, "I just noticed something. Everyone at this table is sad."

"No kidding," said Mom. "I'm so depressed I—I don't know what."

Dad spread a droplet of water around the vinyl tablecloth with his knife. "Some things are just hard to get over. We're trying. But we'll all have to be patient, I guess."

Things weren't working out the way Chelsie had said they would. We should have been talking about happy things.

The woman at the next table couldn't stop laughing at a joke, but Dad and Mom were both dabbing at their eyes with napkins.

The waiter came back to ask if we wanted more coffee. I said, "No, thank you," just to get rid of him.

Mom smiled through red eyes. "Think of something cheerful. I don't like bawling in restaurants."

So we talked about school and Dad's restaurant and a lot more about Heidi Little.

It was drizzly outside. Just walking from the restaurant to the car made you feel damp and horrible. It was perfect weather for depression. But before he unlocked the car doors, Dad gave both Matthew and me a hug, right there on the asphalt.

"It'll take awhile, but we'll all get better. I'm sure God has a plan."

I tried not to notice that he didn't exactly sound as though he believed it.

Well, I had done my best. Now it was God's turn.

# 6

I made my mouth a big "O" and drew on plenty of red. Hmm. Good, but not nearly dramatic enough, I decided, squinting into the mirror propped up on my desk. I added more black to my eyebrows. Not bad. Another smear of orange on the cheeks.

"Who are you supposed to be?" It was Matthew, poking his head into my bedroom, but not coming in.

"Who do you think?"

"I don't know. You're scary. Are you a witch?"

In the mirror I rolled my eyes. Brothers.

"I'm Cleopatra, dummy. Cleopatra was a very sophisticated woman in the olden days. On the Nile

41

and all that. And she wasn't scary."

Then he came in. He sprawled on my bed and watched me silently, chin cupped in his hands.

"It's not Halloween," he pointed out. "In case you hadn't noticed."

"In case you hadn't noticed, I'm practicing to become a star. I'm taking up acting. And since I just watched *Antony and Cleopatra* on the TV movie matinee, I thought I'd start with her."

His mouth dropped open. "You're kidding," he said. "I thought actors had to be tall."

"Models have to be tall, not actors. Matthew, sometimes you really take the cake."

I got up close to the mirror, so I could see my pores, all caked with orange makeup. I looked very theatrical, but not exactly sophisticated. What was missing? False eyelashes, maybe.

Downstairs, the phone rang.

"Would you go get the phone, Matthew, dear?" I said regally, like a star.

He made a move to go, then stopped. "You're just being nice to me because you want me to answer the phone."

Ring two.

I glared at him. "Please, please, please, Matthew. Please go answer the phone? You know I can't go downstairs like this."

"Why not?" he said, raising his eyebrows innocently.

I pointed to my face. "Because Mom and Dad

would kill me if they saw me like this. Not kill me, of course, but—"

Ring three.

"I'll make a deal with you," he said, not sounding innocent anymore. "You make me an ice-cream sundae after I answer the phone, and bring it up to my room, and I'll—"

I didn't have time to listen to the rest of his bargain. I jumped up from my desk and ran downstairs.

"Hello?" I asked in a puffing voice.

"I almost hung up," said a faraway voice I didn't recognize.

"I'm sorry," I said, gasping. "I was upstairs, and Matthew wouldn't answer the phone, and—"

"I'm calling for Roberta Shippley Mahoney. Is she about?"

"Just a second," I said. "I'll get her."

"Quickly, please. This is long distance."

I looked everywhere for her. She wasn't in the yard or upstairs. I figured she and Dad must have gone over to the Johnstons' to talk. They do that sometimes. But I sure wasn't going to trot over there looking like this.

"I'm sorry," I said into the receiver. "She's around, but I can't find her anywhere. Could you call back in an hour?"

There was a long pause.

"Hello?" I asked, thinking she had hung up.

"I'm still here," said the voice. "I'm just think-

ing. No, in an hour I'll be meeting with my agent—
No, I'll have to leave a message. Could you relay it?
By the way, with whom am I speaking?"

"This is Victoria Hope Mahoney," I said,
dignified.

"Oh, *Victoria*." For a second the woman
sounded confused and embarrassed. "I can't believe I didn't recognize your voice. It's changed
since we last spoke. I thought you might be one of
those other people in the commune."

Commune? What commune? Who was this person, anyway?

"This is Isadora Shippley," she said, sounding
embarrassed again. "Your grandmother."

The line crackled and buzzed while I tried to
think of anything at all to say.

"Hello, Grandmother," I said at last, formally.

# 7

It took some scrubbing, but I got most of Cleopatra off my face before Mom and Dad came back from the Johnstons'. When I saw them crossing into our yard I ran out the back door.

"Guess what," I shouted. "You'll never guess who called."

"Tom Selleck," said my mom.

"Insurance salesman?" asked Dad. "Avon? *Reader's Digest* Million-Dollar Sweepstakes chairman?"

"Grandma! Grandma Shippley."

Mom stopped abruptly, one foot on the steps into the house.

"My mother? It couldn't have been my mother."

"Let's go inside." Smoothly, Dad opened the

door and gave us both gentle shoves inside.

Mom started asking a ton of questions. "What did she want? How did she sound? Did she recognize your voice?" The words all ran together.

"Sit down, Bob. Let Vickie get a word in. And I'll pour us some cider."

I plopped into a kitchen chair, trying to remember all the details of the conversation.

"Okay," said Dad. "From the top."

"I didn't have the foggiest who she was," I said slowly, practicing my dramatic voice. "I said hello, and she asked for Mom."

"Yes?" said Mom. "How did she sound?"

I thought it over. "Sort of scared."

"Scared? My mother's not afraid of anything. Her paintings are exhibited all over the country."

I remember the first time Mom told me my grandmother was a painter. I thought it was really terrific. I told my class about her in show and tell the next day. Richie Blodgett said *his* grandmother lived on a farm, and he got to visit her once a month and ride the horses.

"I looked for you guys," I said. "You weren't around. Obviously. I would have just waltzed over and gotten you at the Johnstons', but—well, that's another story."

"Don't tell us," Dad said. "One drama at a time is enough."

"So I asked her to call back in an hour. But she couldn't because—"

46

"—she was going to be busy in her studio," my mother finished.

"Easy." Dad placed three iced glasses of cider on the table.

"Actually, Mom, it was something about her agent."

"Same thing."

"Then she asked who I was."

"You mean she didn't recognize your voice? Her own granddaughter? Her only granddaughter?"

"Mom," I said logically, "I haven't talked to her in at least four years. Not since Great-Aunt Helen's wedding. Remember?"

"How could I forget? Aunt Helen's pretty hard to miss."

All of a sudden I had this memory of the wedding: this crazy brass band booming the wedding march, and Great-Aunt Helen thundering down the aisle.

Dad took a long swallow of cider. "I wonder if she had to have that dress specially made," he mused. "I've never seen so much taffeta in one place."

"I liked Great-Aunt Helen," I said, feeling guilty for snickering. "She had a good sense of humor."

A smirk started at the corners of Mom's mouth. "She had an *immense* sense of humor."

"Gigantic," I agreed.

We started to laugh. We laughed until we got hysterical and Dad put down his cider to keep from

47

spilling it and Mom put her head on the table and just shook. Dad's eyes closed, and he hugged himself as if he were in pain. Laughing had a nice effect on his face. I guess I have always taken laughing for granted.

"Anyway," Mom said, wiping tears from her eyes, "we've established that Aunt Helen's wedding was the last time you talked to your grandmother."

I nodded, remembering shaking my grandmother's hand in the receiving line. It was a big hand. Strong, too. "How good to see you again," she had said, briskly. I could have been the kid down the street.

She was the exact opposite of Great-Aunt Helen, her sister. Aunt Helen was soft and slow. My grandmother was thin and quick. In her high-heeled shoes she towered over everyone. Her hair was gray and cut short, like a boy's. She had on this wild magenta dress, so bright it almost hurt your eyes. After asking me a few questions about school, she turned to the next person in line.

"She was surprised when I said I was me," I continued.

"Well, who did she think you were? The maid?"

"No, someone from the commune. That's what she said, 'commune.'"

Mom and Dad let out puffs of air like deflating balloons.

"Commune!" they said together.

48

"Brother, is she behind!" said Dad. He looked at me. "Once, years ago, before you and Matthew were twinkles in anyone's eyes, we lived in a commune. You know, where people live together and share their belongings."

"Oh, gross, Dad. You mean like everyone wearing babushkas and earth shoes, and eating whole wheat stuff?"

"Well, not exactly," he said. "You take all the romance out of it. The concept of sharing was terrific, even if it wasn't for us. Not too long after that I started cooking school, your mother went back to the university for a degree, we moved into a rattletrap apartment, and that was the end of our commune living."

"What's Grandma talking about, then?"

"My mother," said Mom with a sigh, "doesn't know much about us at all. She simply got busy with her painting and dropped out of sight. The real tragedy is that she doesn't know you and Matthew, the two most adorable children in Minnesota, at all." She put down her glass with force. "The suspense is killing me. What did she want? What possible reason could my mother have for calling?"

I paused dramatically, letting the tension build. All the drama coaches tell you to do that. Then I told them: "She's moving to Minneapolis!"

# 8

Monday mornings roll in like thunder. There's no stopping them.

From my bedroom window I could see Chels coming, so I dashed out to the gate to meet her. She had a raspberry Danish in one hand and she was chomping down on it every few seconds.

How'd she get away with eating Danish for breakfast? My parents would have a stroke. They are real sticklers about well-balanced meals, the four basic food groups, and all that. Mom especially. She's into sprouts and lentil beans.

"How was your weekend?" Chels asked. "I haven't talked to you since our sleep-over. Was my dessert idea a success?"

I had to take long steps to keep up with her. "I don't think my family is in the mood to be cheered up right now," I said. Her face practically fell into her socks, so I added, "It might have worked if we hadn't gotten The Phone Call yesterday."

"What phone call?"

I let her sweat it out just for a minute. I was getting pretty good at this acting stuff.

"What call? What call?" she said, grabbing my arm.

"Remember my grandma, the one I told you about?

"The artist? She called? How come? I thought you never heard from her."

"She's moving here. At least for a while."

"Why?"

I shrugged. "Who knows? Mom thinks to bully her or boss her around or something."

She whistled. "Dragon lady grandmother comes to hassle her kid. That's dramatic. How are your parents taking it?"

"They're kind of nervous."

"Out of the frying pan into the fire."

Chelsie's always using sayings like that. Half the time I hardly know what she's talking about, but of course I can't say that. I have my pride.

"Mom said she doesn't know how much more she can take. I mean, she's too worn out to entertain, of course."

"Well, that changes things. We need a double-whammy plan. It has to cheer your parents up *and* keep your grandma out of their hair. We'll have to distract her, that's what. Get her interested in something else."

"Impossible," I said.

"Where there's a will, there's a way, Vic. Haven't you ever heard that?"

I had. But it didn't help.

I got my feet going at the same rate as hers. We were really clipping along. I could almost feel all the oxygen rushing up to my brain.

"Hey, I know!" I stopped her right there on the sidewalk. "Let's introduce her to eligible bachelors. You know, suitors. *Boyfriends.*"

She looked at me, perfectly still. The light was beginning to dawn. "That's riiight. She's not married, is she?"

"No. Mom's father died when she was little. He was an insurance salesman, and—"

"Spare me the gory details. I just ate a roll, you know. Now, let's see. How many eligible bachelors do we know?"

"There's your Grandpa Bixler."

"Grandpa Bixler? Are you kidding? If we link those two up, we'll just have to come up with a way to keep your grandma from bugging *my* parents. Anyway, Grandpa lives in Tallahassee. We need somebody who lives around here, so he can whisk her away to dinner when she's being a pest."

We walked a ways further.

"I've got it." Chelsie snapped her fingers and stopped dead. "We'll fix her up with Mr. Wilkes!"

Hmm. It was a good plan. Our old friend Harold Wilkes lived in an apartment building close by, and he was eligible, all right. The only trouble was, I liked him. It didn't seem right to sic Grandma on a friend.

"Stop looking so worried, Vic. This'll be a snap. All we do is introduce them, and let nature take over from there. Of course, Mr. Wilkes will have to take up an interest in art and stuff. Maybe he could lose a little weight, too."

"You're forgetting something," I said. "My grandmother is weird. I know, 'cause I've met her. She's not his type."

"You're right. He is a pretty normal guy. Except for the way he's crazy about cats, Mr. Wilkes is your average nice person."

"—And she's definitely not the baking-cookies-and-knitting type of grandmother. I wish she was, but she's not."

"Be grateful you've even got a grandmother. I don't anymore, remember?"

Chelsie's Grandma Warden, who was a very good friend of mine, died last summer. It was terrifically sad, for both Chelsie and me.

Chels made her voice brisk. "Stop thinking of reasons this won't work. We'll make it work. You want to help out your parents, don't you? They couldn't handle much more."

*What about me*, I wanted to say. *I've had to go through a lot, too, you know. It's not easy losing your baby sister.* This incredible sadness came out of nowhere. It put a heaviness like a weight in my chest.

But Chels was talking a mile a minute, and it was hard not to be excited along with her. We could send them each secret notes to get them interested in each other, and then—

We met Peggy and Lynette cutting across the school baseball field. They both had on new spring jackets, one lemon drop yellow, one spring sky blue.

"Hi, you all," called Lynette, using one of Peg's favorite cornball phrases. "We've been yelling at you for three blocks. What are you talking about that's so interesting?"

Chels didn't slow down. She's a fast walker, that's for sure. We all had to chase after her to keep up.

"Vic's grandmother's moving to Minneapolis," she told them. "And we're trying to line her up with an eligible bachelor."

"How about Grant Hirshfield?" said Peg, giggling. Everyone knows Chelsie likes him.

"Not funny," said Chels. "Anyway, we're looking for an older type. The mature type."

"My grandmother lives in Mississippi," said Peggy, "in the same house she was born in. Every time we go there she tells us the same stories about the family history. It's interesting and all, but I've heard it about a hundred times. She also has all kinds of old letters and pictures. Some of that stuff is probably a hundred years old. Two hundred, even."

"Speaking of pictures," said Lynette, "my grandmother shows my picture to everyone. Even strangers on the street. It's *so* embarrassing."

Chelsie told them all about our plan. All the details.

Another Monday. It had started out like just another normal day, but by the time we got to school, we had The Shippley-Wilkes Courtship Plan all figured out.

"Cupids Incorporated, that's what we are," I said, holding the front door open for everyone.

Chels liked that. Before we even got to first period humanities, she was talking about printing up business cards and going into matchmaking as a career.

"Please," I said, "one problem at a time."

"Killjoy," said Chels.

# 9

Scouring powder makes me sneeze. Every time I scrub the tub, I sneeze. Today I dumped powder on my sponge and sneezed three times in a row.

"You okay?" Dad stuck his head around the bathroom door.

"I'd be better if I wasn't always in charge of cleaning the tub around here. Matthew is the dirty one in this family. Why can't he clean it?"

"You have seniority."

I didn't crack a smile.

"Let's take a break, Merry Sunshine." He motioned for me to follow him.

"Oh, I don't know," I said. "I love cleaning the bathroom so much, I don't think I can bear to tear

56

myself away." Sometimes I am a master of sarcasm.

"Meeting. Downstairs. You're invited."

He disappeared, and a second later I heard him knocking on my brother's door. I dried off my hands and joined them. Matthew had been working on a giant clay creation since dinner. There was a hideous multicolored monster standing on his desk. Gross.

The three of us walked down the front stairs together, tallest to shortest. I noticed that I could almost see skin through the hair on top of Dad's head. I had a father old enough to lose his hair?

In the family room, Mom was rocking Bullrush. Our cat likes to be rocked. He's just like a baby that way. The lamplight behind the chair cast a romantic glow over her shoulder. She looked like one of those "you'd-never-know-I-color-my-hair" commercials. But when we got closer, she looked tired. It's funny how you can live with people for years and not notice that they're getting older.

"What's up?" I asked her.

"I just got back from the drugstore with these." She reached over and picked a packet off the coffee table. "Pictures," she said.

Matthew and I both made a dive for them.

"Great!" I said. "What of? Us?"

"Jessica."

I snatched my hand back. Even Matthew had the sense to stop.

"We took them at the hospital, after she was

born," Mom went on calmly. "So we'd remember what she looked like."

I couldn't believe it! Taking pictures of a baby—after she was dead? Horrible. Bullrush, curled in a doughnut shape on Mom's lap, sighed and purred up a storm. I just stared at my mother, shocked. She didn't seem to notice.

"We weren't going to take them at first. Then a nurse said we might be sorry later if we didn't. We talked it over, and decided to go ahead. We figured that if we didn't feel we could look at them later, we wouldn't have to."

"I want to see them," Matthew said. "I always wondered what that sister of mine looked like . . . my other sister, that is."

Dad put his arm around my shoulder. "Listen, if you don't want to look, you don't have to. Okay?"

"It's no big deal," I snapped. I was angry, burning angry.

Everyone moved to the couch. I let Matthew wedge between Mom and Dad. I sort of leaned over them all. That way I could duck out quick if anything got too gross.

The first picture: someone's arms were holding a bundle. The smallest, roundest face in the world was showing between the big folds of cloth. I was totally surprised. She looked like a normal baby. Her puffy eyes were closed. Just a ducktail of orange hair showed on her forehead. She looked like she was sleeping. Jessica.

"That's her?" asked Matthew. "I can hardly believe it."

"Why?" Mom was smiling. "Why can you hardly believe it?"

"She's so cute."

"What did you expect?" Dad grinned at Matthew, too, and stroked his hair.

The second picture was of the baby in a yellow sleeper suit. The sleeper was huge compared to Jessica. She was on a bed. Her arms were out, and her fingers were curled. She looked like any second someone would pick her up and bundle her into the car for the drive home from the hospital.

The next picture was of Mom holding Jessica. Mom was not smiling.

Dad looked up at me. He was analyzing my expression, I could tell. I tried to look as bored as I probably do in Mrs. Hartford's math class, but it was no use.

"This upsetting you?" he asked.

"No, of course not," I said, in a tone that usually gets me in trouble for sassing.

Everybody kept saying how cute she had been and how glad they were they had taken the pictures, but I thought the whole thing was gross and disgusting.

Mom was flipping through a Bible, finding that verse that everyone keeps using, the one about all things working together for good. I, for one, was sick of hearing it. I just didn't see how good could come out of something awful. If God wanted good things to happen, why didn't he just skip right over the sad stuff? He could allow a lot more wonderful things to happen—things that wouldn't be as complicated to work out. If anyone used that old line on me again, I'd let 'em have it. And that included the pastor.

"—it's hard to see how he can do it," Mom was saying, "but here it is, his promise. Somehow that's comforting. We know that sometime we'll be able to say, 'Yeah, that was horrible, but something worthwhile did come out of it.' "

She said she couldn't wait until that happened. And then tears blurred up her eyes. Or maybe they were my eyes. I wasn't sure.

# 10

We have this very peculiar mailman. He looks as
if he hasn't had a good meal in ages, he's so thin.
His hair is pure white. But he's sharp, all right,
sharp as a tack. When I am outside he always
delivers the mail to me personally. "Love letters for
you, miss," he says with a super-straight face.

I thought this was funny till last fall, when I had a
real-life experience with love letters. I got them
from a guy at school named Corey, but they were
really sent as a joke by a girl named Hilary who was
jealous of me or something. It's a long story.
Anyway, whenever I hear "love letters" now, that's
what I think of, and I get a massive pain in the
stomach. I don't care if I ever get another.

I was helping Matthew find his rusty old roller skates in the garage, when the mailman arrived.

"More love letters for you, miss," he said, sifting quickly through a bunch of envelopes without cracking a smile. "Quite a stack."

I didn't smile either. I held out my hand. "Thank you, Theodore," I said, as if this happened to me all the time. Theodore is not his name, but that's what I call him.

"Just doing my job," he said, starting to sort more envelopes. "I'll have countless more for you tomorrow." He headed back down the sidewalk.

"Come on," whined Matthew, digging under a pile of dirty old plastic. "I'll never find 'em if you don't help."

"Okay, okay. Just a sec—"

Then, right there in the stack, I found the envelope. "Hold it a minute, Matthew. This is a very important letter. I've got to take it to Mom."

I went to the front door and yelled. "Mom!"

She came from the basement, scowling at me. "Next time come and get me. I don't appreciate being called for like the neighborhood dog."

I blushed. "Sorry, Mom, but I absolutely pan-icked. I'm not sure, but I think this is the letter we've been waiting for."

Importantly, I held out the long envelope on my open palms, like a butler delivering bonbons.

"It is," said Mom, covering her eyes with her hand. "I can't look. You read it."

She followed me back outside into the sunlight. We sat with our backs against the steps and our knees under our chins.

"Yep," I said. "It's from your mom. Here's her name, right here. Isadora Shippley."

"What does she say?"

I cleared my throat.

" 'Dear Roberta and Terrence,' " I read aloud. "That's good, isn't it? She called you *dear*."

Mom leaned her head against her crossed arms and groaned. "*Roberta*. And *Terrence*. No one calls us that." She pulled herself together. "Okay. I'm fine. Go ahead."

I squinted at the letter and finally made out the next part:

> *This is to confirm the plans I estab-*
> *lished tentatively with Victoria.*

I whistled, the way Chelsie would have. "She uses big words," I said.

"Go on, go on."

> *I will be arriving by bus next Thurs-*
> *day at 8 p.m. Please don't concern*
> *yourselves with picking me up. I'll*
> *take a taxi. I hope I still recognize*
> *you all. And vice versa. Four years is*
> *a long time.*
>
> *Cordially, Isadora Shippley*

"Isadora?" I said, looking up. "Shouldn't she have signed it Mom or Grandma or something?"

Mom shrugged and took the letter from me to

study it carefully. "Well, I guess it's official. She's really coming. What will we talk about? We have nothing in common."

"Maybe things will go better than you think. I have a feeling they might." It was too early to tell her the details of Chelsie's great plan. It'd be a surprise.

She stood up, slapping dust out of her pants. "One thing for sure: she can't stay here. For a few days, of course, but if this is going to be a long stay, it would be better if she had her own place."

"Hotels are expensive," I said.

"I know. Got any better ideas? Are there any apartment buildings around?"

It was so obvious, it was like lightning. "Mr. Wilkes!" I yelled.

"Huh? Why are you shrieking about Mr. Wilkes?"

"He lives in this great apartment building. It always has vacancies."

"I'll call right this minute. What's the place called?"

Things were really going to work out the way Chelsie had said. It was too, too perfect.

# 11

When the splattered silver bus slid into the depot, Mom and Dad both looked at their watches and said, "Right on time," and they didn't sound too happy about it. They sounded nervous.

The bus stopped with a squeal of brakes, sighed, and slapped open its doors.

The first passengers stepped off. First came a lady wearing a very quiet khaki-colored suit and a plain brown coat. I knew that wasn't my grandmother. Next was a man wearing a parka and a stocking cap. All of us shifted from foot to foot. I think we were nervous.

After a long line of people had streamed out, a tall woman appeared and stood for a second on the bottom step of the bus. It was my grandmother.

Her hair had grown out; it was about the same length as Chelsie's new cut, but it was spiky on the ends and gray. She was wearing a purple cape, and one edge was slung grandly over her shoulder. She clutched a huge, brilliant, yellow bag by the handle.

"Let's go," said Mom, giving me a push. We all filed out into the dark, one after another.

"There you are," said my grandmother, stepping down as we all crowded around. "I didn't want you to come all the way out here, but now that you're here, I'm so glad you came. There's nothing worse than a strange bus station in a strange new place."

"Hello, Mother," said Mom, very, very politely. "Glad you made it safely." She sounded as though she were talking to a stranger.

"Hello, Mrs. Shippley," said my dad, also polite.

Matthew didn't say anything at all. Sometimes that kid is pretty smart. I clamped my mouth shut, too. Sometimes it's a good idea just to wait and see how things develop.

Grandmother kind of fiddled with her purse and studied the fine print on her ticket stub. We all fumbled around, that awkward fumbling you do when you don't know whether to hug or not. Matthew is normally a real huggable kid, but he just stood there twisting the string on his jacket hood.

Grandmother smelled like a million—like some

exotic cologne I'd never smelled before. That, plus the jangly earrings, big old cape, and crazy hair sure didn't make her look like anyone's grandmother. She said, "I hope this isn't too much of an inconvenience, my just appearing like this."

"Oh, no, no." Mom and Dad muttered the things adults mutter.

Grandma slapped her hands together and rubbed them. "Then I suppose we should collect my things."

We all made a dive for her luggage. There were enough parcels to load everyone down: suitcases, bags, satchels, briefcases. She had a ton of them. It looked like she was moving in.

"I brought nearly everything I own," she said as we struggled toward the car, "since I didn't know how long I'd be staying. Just my furniture's in storage."

We all piled into the car, with Grandma by the window in the backseat. There was barely room for my legs, with all the boxes and things shoved on the floor. The car turned us back toward downtown Minneapolis.

I have noticed that cities are prettier in the dark. People rush along in the dark, stoplights change colors like blinking Christmas lights. We drove slowly. The only person talking much was Dad. He was chattering away, which he sometimes does when he's nervous.

"Minneapolis isn't exactly what you're used to, is

67

it, Mrs. Shippley? What with all your travels to exciting places."

"Oh, as far as towns go, Minneapolis is okay by me," she answered. "When Roberta was a girl, her father and I would bring her here to see Dayton's Christmas windows. Memories like that are golden."

"I remember that!" said Mom. "They used to set up Christmas scenes in the sales windows—Alice in Wonderland or Santa's workshop. A different one every year."

"We always made a day of it. Shopping, lunch at Peter's Grill. We always ordered apple pie, remember, Roberta?"

"Those were the days before I knew what terrible things sugar does to your system."

"It always snowed, but that was part of the magic."

Dad pointed. "Over there's the IDS Tower. Used to be you could ride up to the top and look out over the whole city. That was before they closed the observation deck. We're on Hennepin Avenue now, heading toward the Mississippi."

We rumbled over the bridge in silence. The tension inside the car started to build again. Since I was sitting by a window I could look down into the dark water below. I learned once in social studies that the Mississippi curls through Minnesota and keeps right on flowing until it reaches the Gulf of Mexico. I wondered how long it would take the water I was seeing tonight to get all the way to the ocean.

Suddenly Dad broke into "Old Man River" in a deep pretend-opera voice.

I could have died. For once, Mom was a little embarrassed, too. I could see red creeping up her neck. But my grandmother started blasting out the alto part, right along with him.

"Terrence, you're a pip, you really are," she said, slapping one skinny knee. I have a feeling I'm going to enjoy living—er, visiting here." She started digging in that yellow bag. "You might as well know Helen tried to talk me out of coming. She said I was meddling." She pulled a glasses case from her bag. She jammed the glasses on and turned to give me a piercing look. "But I told her to mind her own business. To tell the truth, I was lonely. I finally said to myself, 'Isadora, it's time you got to know your family again.' So here I am."

"That's fine, Mom," said my mother, turning. "We're glad to see you. But this is a big switch for us; it'll take some getting used to."

"I know, I know. I'm a little shocked myself. But I know we'll all hit it right off. I'm sure of it." She gave Matthew and me a wink. "Right, kids?"

"Right," I said in a small voice.

Before too long we were pulling into our familiar old driveway.

"So you live in a house," said Grandmother. "How did I get it in my head that you were still in a commune? We have been out of touch for a while. My! This has possibilities, doesn't it? Think of the fabulous studio you could put into a house like this. All that northern exposure."

I climbed out of the car. "May I carry that bag for you, Grandmother?" I asked in a voice that had tons of etiquette in it.

"Oh, Victoria, my dear," she said, laughing. "Call me Isadora, won't you?"

# 12

Isadora got my brother's bedroom, so Matthew got bumped to the family room.

"I get to sleep on the couch!" Matthew screamed at me, when I came downstairs to call Chels. He jumped up and down on the fresh-made bed like a monkey, scratching his armpits. If Mom had seen him leaping around on the couch like that, he'd have been in tons of trouble.

"You better settle down," I told him. "If I were you I'd be quiet as a mouse, down here all by myself. Not that I'd sleep down here all alone. In the dark. By myself. No, sir. Not in a million years."

"I'm not scared," he said, but he quit jumping.

"Just don't come crying to me when you start hearing creepy noises—like footsteps coming up the basement stairs."

His eyes bugged out. He flopped down and snapped the sheets up to his nostrils. "What footsteps?"

"Goodnight, brother, dear," I said. "I'm going to make one very short phone call, and then I'm going to turn off all the lights and go upstairs. Sleep tight."

"Mom!" Matthew started to yell, breaking all volume records. "Mom!"

The great thing about best friends is you never have to say, "This is your friend Victoria," when you call. You also don't have to look up the telephone number.

"What are you doing?" I asked, when Chelsie picked up the phone.

"Emoting," she said. "That's kind of like acting, but with lots more emotion. Emoting, emotion. Get it?"

"I get it. Why are you emoting?"

"Mr. Snow just announced auditions for *Romeo and Juliet*, the play Keats is putting on in May." Her voice turned disgusted. "Everyone in the whole school wanted to do *Brigadoon* except these two snobby ninth graders. They railroaded it through. Anyway, I'm practicing. I made up this alphabetical list of emotions, and I'm going to practice every single one. Indignation. That's next."

"Well, good luck," I said, getting this funny twinge. *I* wanted to be in that show! Maybe even play Juliet, depending on who was Romeo. Victoria Mahoney, star. Maybe I should practice emoting, too. It was worth a try. I'd start right after I hung up.

Next I told her all about my grandma, including the yellow bag and having to call her Isadora.

"Will she be a good match for Mr. Wilkes?" Chels wanted to know.

I tried to imagine the two of them walking arm in arm to the park for a romantic evening together. All I could picture was Mr. Wilkes tripping on her big cape, and Isadora bumping into his big stomach.

"I think," I said, "this is going to be harder than we thought."

"You're just being pessimistic. Hey! Pessimism should be on my list!" There was a pause while she wrote it down. "Anyway, did you find out how long she's staying?"

"All week. Then it's to The Towers with her!"

"Vic, that wasn't bad, not bad at all. Have you ever considered an acting career?"

"Maybe and maybe not," I said mysteriously. "All I can say is there might be one extra person at auditions next time around."

"You? Really? I can see the marquee now: 'Shy Vic, star of stage and screen, here tonight.' "

"Sarcasm," I said. "You're being sarcastic."

"Sarcasm! Great! Let me get that down."

After we said good-bye, I slapped off the kitchen lights and dashed up the stairs to bed. At the top of the first flight, I bumped into something—hard.

"Oof!" I said.

"Oof!" said someone, dropping a toothbrush.

It was Isadora. My blood dropped to a temperature somewhere around zero. "I'm sorry," I said.

She brushed the lint off her toothbrush. "You knocked the wind out of me."

"I'm really sorry," I said again, idiotically. *This is it*, I thought, expecting her to really let me have it.

"We'll both have to be more careful coming around that corner, I guess." She gave a little laugh.

She was wearing these crazy flannel pajamas. They had huge daisies on them—one on the top and one wrapped around a leg. I'd never seen any pj's like them.

"As long as you're here," she said, "I do have a question." She motioned me into Matthew's room. It was crowded with her stuff, and I had to watch where I was going. "Could you find me a mousetrap somewhere? I don't want to insult your parents, but I'm sure I saw something move in here. I was turning down the covers, and out of the corner of my eye, I definitely saw something move over there by my suitcase."

Either the place was haunted or she was crazy.

74

"We haven't had a mouse in months," I said, emoting a great deal of dignity. It would have been rude to call her crazy.

"There!" she shrieked. "There it is again!"

I whipped around, following the angle of her pointing finger.

"My peripheral vision is perfect," she said, standing very still. "The pesky critter is there. Behind the toy box."

I inched over slowly. Stiffly, I bent over and—an orange blur jumped straight toward me, landing precisely on the toy box. It sat blinking its orange eyes and twitching its long, striped tail.

"Bullrush!" I said. "You scared me!"

"My heart," said Isadora, putting her hand on her chest. "I didn't know you had a cat."

"He likes company," I explained. "Actually, he likes their suitcases. He waits until their backs are turned and then he crawls in with the clothes."

"What a fright," she said.

"He usually sleeps with me. I'll take him to my room."

But when I reached for him, she said, "Oh, no, you don't. I adore cats. Leave him right here. I'm the guest, you know, so you have to."

Well, anyone who likes cats can't be all bad, as my dad says. I leaned down to brush my face against Bullrush's bewhiskered, purring one. Then I said good night to my grandmother.

Isadora, that is.

# 13

"Have you seen it, have you seen it?" Chels practically knocked me over in the hallway outside of my home ec class.

I was in a bad mood. Home ec always puts me in a bad mood. So I just gave her a semisour look and said, "Seen what?"

"There's a sign-up sheet for *Romeo and Juliet* tryouts outside the auditorium. Come and look."

She led the way to the auditorium. "There!" she said proudly, pointing out her name next to the number five.

"That doesn't look like your handwriting," I said.

"It's my new penmanship. It's all part of developing a stage presence, you know."

"Oh." We stared at the board, and I started giving myself a silent pep talk. *Your name could be up there, too,* I told myself firmly. *You, too, could be a superstar. It's now or never. Go for it.*

"Do you have a pen?" I asked Chelsie casually.

"Sure," she said, feeling for one in her purse. "Why?"

Before I could change my mind I made my hand write out my name, right next to the six. It came out in my normal handwriting, but it was up there.

Chelsie didn't scream or jump up and down or anything. She just shook her head. "Never thought I'd see the day. Are you sure you know what you're doing?"

"Maybe I'd like to try being a star, too."

"What about the writing?"

"I'll do both."

"I just want you to remember that acting takes guts, Vic, old pal. Don't come crying to me."

I made a face. "See this?" I said, pointing at my expression. "I'm emoting hurt feelings. And I'm not faking."

"I'm sorry. Listen, if you want to give it a try, I'll even help you practice. Want to come over tonight? After school?"

"Sure! Yeah!"

"I'll make you work hard," she warned. "Thespians have a hard life."

"Huh?"

She sighed and motioned for me to walk back to

77

class with her. "Vic, before you start your brilliant acting career, you sure have a lot to learn."

She was right. The sooner I got started, the better.

"Meet me after school," I said. "Two-fifty-five sharp."

I had my locker open and my coat on before she even showed.

"Brett Tarvick wanted to talk," she said, giggling and messing with her combination. "He's so weird."

I could tell by the way she said weird she didn't mean weird at all. I sighed and held my books closer.

On the walk home Chels told me about her progress on the courtship plan. "I told Mr. Wilkes that your grandma was in town. Shy and demure. That's how I described her."

"Shy?" I asked. "I don't think that's quite the word for my grandma."

"Well, what did you want me to tell him? That she carries a yellow purse and sings opera? Be realistic."

"Tell him she's wild about cats. She is."

"Perfect. We'll get him to invite her over to meet Penzance."

Penzance is the cat that lives with Mr. Wilkes. He bought her as a favor to Chelsie, because her parents wouldn't let her have one.

We had to stop at my house to ask if I could go over to Chelsie's. Matthew, of course, was in his usual spot by the TV. Mom and Isadora were standing in the backyard. They both looked relieved to see us, like people at a party who have run out of things to say to each other.

Mom handled the introductions. I appreciated that because I always forget who's supposed to be introduced to whom, first.

"Call me Isadora," said my grandmother, pumping Chelsie's hand off.

Chelsie didn't miss a beat. "I've heard all about you, ma'am," she said. "Vic says that you—"

"We have to go," I said, dragging Chelsie by the arm. "We're going over to her house to practice emoting. See you."

"It's in the bag," said Chels in a whisper, once we got outside. "She's Mr. Wilkes's type all right."

"How could you tell?"

"You can't explain intuition, Vic. You just have to trust it."

All I can say is that it's terrible when your best friend not only has all kinds of acting talent, but intuition, too.

# 14

"What's this grandma of yours like?" Mr. Wilkes asked.

He was demonstrating soap carving for us at his apartment. There were soap shavings everywhere, and the room smelled like a bath.

Across the table, Chels and I exchanged nervous looks.

"She's sort of—" I paused, trying to think up the right word, one that would bring out her positive traits.

"—artistic," Chels finished for me. "She's just the kind of person who'd love to take your hand-crafts class at the senior citizens' club. I have this intuition that she's really into soap carving."

80

Somehow I couldn't picture it.

In the kitchen, the teapot started whistling wildly. Mr. Wilkes got up, and Penzance jumped onto the warm seat, curling her tail around herself and closing her eyes.

"So far, so good," Chels whispered.

I still had my doubts.

He came back with three steaming cups on a tray, and an assortment of tea bags. I picked out a spicy orange one and dipped it in my cup until the steam was fragrant and the water turned a deep golden color. Mr. Wilkes delicately placed Penzance on the floor and picked up the soap again.

"And she's moving into The Towers?" he asked.

"We wanted her to have her own place," I explained, "because she may be around for months."

"Years, even," Chelsie added.

This wasn't very subtle, but I decided to try it anyway. "She's crazy about cats, just like you."

"Mmm?"

"And she'll be moving in this weekend."

"Mmm?"

"So if you want to go say hi to her, this weekend would be a good time. She'll probably be very lonely all by herself."

"Hand me that knife there, will you?"

I did. Then I made a hopeless face at Chelsie. Our no-fail courtship plan was bombing.

She started jerking her head toward the door.

81

"Chelsie," said Mr. Wilkes, looking up for the first time, "are you all right? Do you have a kink in your neck?"

"Mr. Wilkes," I said, trying to save her. "We have to . . . um . . . go blow our noses."

We headed to the bathroom. Chelsie locked the door and turned on the fan. I blew my nose on some toilet paper.

"Great," I said, muffled because of the toilet paper. "He's probably supersuspicious now, but I didn't know what else to do."

"He doesn't seem too interested, does he?" Chelsie pulled a comb out of her pocket. Even though her hair didn't need it, she combed it. She left black hairs all over the sink.

"We've got to do something drastic." She paused, leaning toward the mirror for suspense. "We've got to get her over here. Maybe if he meets her, she'll charm the socks off him."

"Oh, boy," I said, rolling my eyes. "Are you forgetting how strange she is? He'll probably think she's so weird he won't even speak to her."

"Okay, so Mr. Wilkes can do the charming. But first we've got to get her over here."

"Easier said than done." This is one of my mother's favorite phrases. "We'd better go back out there before he gets even more suspicious."

There were voices coming from the kitchen, familiar voices. One was Mr. Wilkes's.

"I just stopped by to meet your cat," said the

other. "The lady in 2206 said you had one, and since I'm going to be moving in down the hall this weekend—"

"Isadora!" I said.

She was standing there in a crazy paint-splashed sweat shirt. It looked like it had been splashed on purpose, and it was about a hundred sizes too big. Her jeans had holes in the knees. The yellow bag was slung over one shoulder. Mr. Wilkes was staring at her as if she were from Mars.

"This is my gr—Isadora," I stuttered. "And this is Mr. Wilkes, a friend of mine."

"Pleased," she said, giving him the old strong arm.

"Same here. Girls have been telling me about you. Said you're interested in crafts."

"Crafts?" Isadora's head went back, and she gave a loud laugh. It wasn't a petite, grandmotherly one, either; it was her crazy lady laugh, the one she had laughed at Dad's opera music.

"No, I'm sorry. I'm not interested in crafts, exactly. I'm interested in art. I'm a painter."

I have never seen Mr. Wilkes blush before, but that's what he did. Under his white hair, his skin went red. The more she talked about fine art and exhibiting in galleries, the redder he got.

"Mr. Wilkes teaches a class at the senior citizens' club," I said, feeling sorry we had ever thought of matching up the two of them.

"Do you?" Isadora asked him, with a nice smile.

I looked at Chelsie, and she looked at me, and we groaned together, very softly. Luckily the cat came out of hiding about then, and Isadora leaned over to pet her. Penzance loved the attention. She jumped up on the table, scattering soap shavings.

We all paused, waiting for her to stop petting the cat. It was nerve racking, very nerve racking. Only Penzance seemed happy.

"Well," Isadora said at last. "Guess I'll be off."

"Nice meeting you," Mr. Wilkes said. He didn't try to talk her into staying for a cup of tea.

# 15

There was this really great show on the educational channel, a real silent movie.

"Do we have to watch this?" Matthew asked. "I'm bored." He started showing off, pulling his head through his T-shirt so that only the top of his head showed. Very funny.

Mom, who was polishing old brass door hinges over spread newspaper, said, "There aren't supposed to be any words, Matthew. This was made before there was sound in movies. You have to watch the action."

Matthew groaned and rolled onto his back with his arms and legs sticking into the air like a dead cat's. Little kids don't appreciate history. I went back to taking notes. There was a lot of stuff I wanted to remember for my audition.

The story was about a beautiful orphan who moves from an orphanage in Boston to scratch out a miserable life of poverty in New York City. After months and months, she meets this kind old man who treats her like a daughter, for no reason at all, just to be nice. He brings her oranges and little gifts, but she won't take money. She's too proud.

Sometimes, to pay him back for his kindness, she cooks him meals. He doesn't mind her grubby little apartment, even though he is very rich. Finally he convinces her to let him buy her a little laundry shop so she can earn a living. She works her head off.

One day the old man's mean maid comes in. She doesn't like doing laundry, so she brings in all his shirts. "Wash these," she says with a nasty sneer. "And they had better be spotless!" (You had to read this on the screen, because of it being a silent movie.)

The orphan girl is so good and sweet that of course she starts doing them. Then, in one of the pockets she finds a letter from a Boston orphanage, the one she left. The letter says they have finally tracked down his long-lost daughter, Blossom, to somewhere in New York!!! Then she knows that the kind man is really her father, who's been searching for her for years, ever since they were separated in some Great Flood or other. I cried my eyes out.

Mom didn't cry. I couldn't figure it out, because she has been crying a lot since Jessica died. She just kept polishing. "That was melodrama with a capital M," she said.

"I found it extremely sad," I said in a dramatic way. "It was sensitive."

"It was boring." Matthew was still doing acrobatics on the couch.

Mom squinted at my notebook. "Reminds me. Didn't I once say no television during homework?"

"Homework!" I snorted snobbishly. "This isn't homework. It's notes about acting."

"Boy," said Matthew. "You're not even *in* the play and already you think you're a star."

I closed my eyes. *It's the night of my first movie premiere. I'm in a dress made all of sequins. Gold sequins. The crowd is going wild. From the back of a white Cadillac, I'm waving. "I love you all!" I'm shouting in a voice that has just a hint of an English accent.*

Clomping footsteps on the staircase interrupted my dream. Oh, boy. Isadora in her clogs again. I opened my eyes.

"Hi, Isadora," said my dumb brother, as if he hadn't seen her for days. Actually it had been about fifteen minutes.

She spread her arms and spun around. "What do you think of this?" she asked. She was wearing a green shirt that hung clear to her knees. Her pants were black, and so tight you could tell how skinny

87

she was. A huge turquoise necklace hung around her neck.

"The shirt's straight from Peking," she informed us. "Genuine silk. What do you think if I wear it tonight? Does it need a belt?"

I was frozen to the carpeting. Tonight was the night Isadora was taking us out for a Mexican dinner. She was going to wear *that*?

"It's lovely," I heard Mom say.

I twisted around to glare at her. She looked as though she meant it, which was worse.

Isadora gave her a grateful look. "Okay, I'll wear it." She swirled out of the room, and her clogs banged back up the stairs.

"Wait!" Matthew took off after her.

I gave my mother The Look. She didn't notice right away. Finally she glanced up.

"What?" she said in an unconcerned voice.

"How could you tell Isadora to wear that? How *could* you? I'm absolutely furious!"

She went back to polishing. "What's wrong with the outfit? It looked all right to me."

I narrowed my eyes and spit the words out like poison. "I cannot be seen in public with Isadora. Not if she's going to wear silly clothes."

"Of all the ridiculous—I knew this would happen when you got to be a teenager. I just knew it." Now Mom was attacking the hinge.

"If Isadora goes, I'm not," I said, crossing my arms for emphasis.

88

Mom threw down the rag. "Victoria Hope Mahoney, I can't believe you could be so petty and intolerant. It doesn't matter what your grandmother wears to dinner. *You* can wear whatever you like."

Mom doesn't get mad that often, but she had almost polished all the finish off that hinge. "Turn off that TV," she said. "You've learned enough about acting for one day. Now go upstairs and make sure Matthew's not into any trouble. He's too quiet."

"Why me?" I knew I was on dangerous ground, but I said it anyway.

"Because."

I glared at her, but this time when she looked up, she glared back. I decided I'd better go upstairs. Quickly.

I trudged resentfully up the stairs, emoting like crazy. Matthew's room is the first room on the right. I knocked.

There was a noise like a can tipping over. Matthew giggled, and Isadora's voice said, "Yes, who is it?"

"It's me. Vickie."

The door opened. Isadora was standing there in the green shirt. The sleeves were rolled up, and there were fresh specks of paint all over the front. She had a bandanna over her hair.

"We're creating," Matthew called from inside.

"Sshh. You'll give away our secret." Then she

leveled a look at me. "I suppose it would have come out sooner or later."

She stepped aside and let me enter.

I couldn't believe it. I looked around with my mouth practically hanging open. There was no polite way to put it, so I just blurted it flat out: "It looks like a bomb exploded in here."

The furniture was pushed back, and there was newspaper all over the floor. A canvas was propped up against the wall, and another was wedged upright between two suitcases. There were brushes and jars of colored water everywhere. I stepped closer to the canvas and almost stepped on a tube of paint on the floor.

"What's going on in here?" I asked, sounding like an adult. Like a parent, almost.

"Painting," said Isadora in an exasperated voice. "What else?"

"Shut the door, shut the door," said Matthew, bouncing on the bed.

Isadora grabbed my arm and pulled me into the room. Then she closed the door—slammed it is more like it.

"You're not here to spy on us, are you?"

I shook my head, trying to see around her shoulder. "What are you painting?"

She flashed a grin over at my brother. "This and that. Odd little projects. Want to see?"

"Sure."

"Okay. Ready? You probably won't like it." She

picked up the canvas and turned it for me to see. "Voilá."

It was a painting of a boy—no, it was a girl. She was in a blur, as if she were moving or standing in a mist. You wanted to blink to clear the mist. I did blink, but the girl stayed hidden in the fog, looking out curiously. She was chubby—young, maybe three years old. Her hair was a glossy golden red that just tickled the tops of her ears. Her eyes looked sleepy, and one side of her hair was sticking up a bit, as if she'd just gotten up. She was wearing something white and filmy, like old-fashioned eyelet or embroidery.

"Who is she?" I asked.

"Oh, a combination of people. There's even a little of you and Matthew in her."

I stared hard at the picture. *Me?* Not even close.

"My hair's different."

Isadora was impatient again. "As I just said, she's many people. It's not supposed to be a portrait. You were her inspiration, not her model." She put her hand out suddenly and lifted my chin. "You have a paintable face. I noticed for the first time at the bus depot." Then she vigorously rubbed at my skin with her thumb. "Just a dot of blue there."

She let me hold the canvas by its edges and look at the painting closely. I couldn't believe anyone could actually paint like this. Whenever I try to draw I end up starting over about a thousand times and I never do get it right.

91

Isadora scratched at some flecks of paint on her shirt. "But I don't have any of the right tools. Why didn't I at least bring my easel?"

"Mr. Wilkes has an easel. He uses it for his craft class. I bet he'd let you use it once you move in at The Towers."

I had some homework to do, so I excused myself. Isadora escorted me to the door as if I were a visitor to an art museum—as if I couldn't be trusted to leave without breaking something.

"Don't tell your mother about this," she ordered in a whisper, at the door. "Messes worry her. Besides, it'll all be cleaned up by the time I leave Saturday."

"Um . . . did you know there's paint on your new shirt?" I asked.

"This thing? Yes. Makes a nice painting shirt. I decided it wasn't flamboyant enough for dinner out, but never fear. I have another outfit that will be just right for the occasion."

She closed the door behind me.

# 16

The sign outside the auditorium screamed at me in big orange letters.
AUDITIONS TONIGHT!
4:00 P.M.!!
BE THERE!!!
That was only six hours away. Suddenly my hands were slippery, and my throat was tight. I put my hand to my head. Maybe I had a fever. The school nurse would have to call my mom, who would have to come pick me up. Then I'd go home and lie in bed moaning.

I got jabbed from behind.

"Hi, Vickie." It was Peggy Hiltshire, big, perfect smile and all. "You going to try out? I never thought you would try out for a play. I guess you're not as shy as I thought. I'm going to try out, too."

She probably wanted to try out because she thought Juliet would get to kiss Romeo.

"How long do auditions take?" I asked her.

"Well, we each get three minutes to do something dramatic. I'm going to sing and act. My parents have this record of *Brigadoon*. I memorized a song. The actors even talked on the record, and I'm going to do it just like them. Want to hear it?"

People on their way to class turned and gaped as Peggy gave it her all right there in the hallway. It was pretty good, except for her accent, which sounded more southern than Scottish. After the second chorus, I said I had to get going.

"See you later," she said, waving.

I dodged back toward where I had last seen Chelsie—by her locker. She was still there, talking to Charita.

"Okay, what's wrong?" she asked immediately. "I can tell something's up."

"I can't do it," I croaked.

"Excuse me a minute, Charita. Now, Vic, what'd you say? Speak up."

"I can't audition."

"WHAT DO YOU MEAN, YOU CAN'T AUDITION? I'VE BEEN PRACTICING WITH YOU FOR WEEKS!"

"I'm scared!" I said, getting my voice back suddenly.

"Oh." She relaxed. "Is that all? Vic, all actors get the jitters. It's normal."

It didn't feel normal. It felt gross.

"Try breathing deeply. Pretend you're on a deserted island. It's just you and the palm trees and the monkeys—"

"It's not working," I said, opening my eyes. "I'm still petrified."

Chelsie gave her locker door a push. "If you chicken out now, you'll never forgive yourself. Trust me."

"Trust you? You? You're the one who talked me into buying those artificial fingernails, remember? My real ones were practically poisoned by the glue."

"You've got to admit they were cool while they lasted. Especially after we painted them with that baby blue polish."

"I might try that," said Charita, looking at her short nails critically.

"I'll bomb," I said, gloomily. "I know it."

Charita gave me a little punch in the arm. "You can do it, kid."

"Be there," Chels called, turning to go.

The place was packed out. They were all kids I didn't know, eighth and ninth graders mostly, and no Chelsie in sight. Everyone looked talented. I picked at the fabric on the auditorium seat. I was the only nervous kid there.

Then I saw a familiar face. Peter! He was crouched on a step near the stage, almost invisible. I sneaked over.

"What are you doing?" I whispered, making him jump.

"Get down," he said, yanking on my shirt. "I'm hiding out. I can't decide if I should try out or not."

"Why not?"

"Heard rumors. Mr. Snow threatened to make all the guys try on tights. He wants to know if they'd look like nerds in them."

Nervous as I was, I snickered. I used to think Peter was a potential boyfriend. But now we're just plain friends. It's funny when you find out you can be friends with a guy, as if he were a normal person.

"Besides," he went on, "I get stage fright like crazy."

"Then why try out?"

"My dad. He's an actor, part-time, when he's not teaching. He thinks it would be good for me."

Peter's dad is divorced. Sometimes I think old Peter babies him, just so his dad's feelings won't be hurt. You have to think of things like that when your parents are divorced.

"What's wrong with you? You look—" he peered into my face—"kind of sickly."

96

"Thanks," I said. "I'm not sick, I'm scared. I'm supposed to be trying out, too. Only I've got stage fright, if that's what you call it. And I promised Chelsie I'd try out. If I don't, she'll think I'm a quitter."

Mr. Snow was standing up on the stage. He blew his stupid whistle and started screaming for people to take their places.

Peter gave me a nudge.

"I know how we can get out of this jam," he said with a sly smile. "Want to hear my backup plan?"

# 17

"I'm in! I'm in like Flynn!"

That's how I announced the big news when I came through the front door. A stampede started, with Matthew coming in first.

"What does that mean?" he asked, puffing.

I removed my jacket, regally. "It's acting talk. It means I made it into the play."

"She's in." Matthew screamed, when Mom flew out from the kitchen, "—like a fin."

"Congratulations!" Mom really looked pleased. She squeezed me until I yelped for air.

"Will wonders never cease?" asked a voice behind me. "Not that I'm surprised, not in the least. The Shippleys have a history of artistic talent." It was Isadora, coming out from the kitchen, wiping grimy hands. I hadn't seen her since her move to the apartment. Even in her latest getup, I was glad to see her, a little. She looked pretty happy to see me, too.

"Come in the kitchen," Mom said, finally releasing me. "You can tell us all about it. We're in the middle of a project."

The stove had been taken apart. There were tools and bits of stove spread all over the floor.

"Looks bad, doesn't it? Never fear, I'll get it back together. Your grandmother's helping."

"Really?" I asked. "Isadora?"

"I'm no slouch with a screwdriver, you know," Isadora said indignantly, giving a stove part a push with the point of her shoe. "And I've never been afraid of a little handiwork. Someday I'll tell you all about my firsthand experiences with a V-8 engine. But first tell us your news. You're entering the exciting world of the theater?"

"Let me kiss your hand," said Matthew, grabbing me.

"Cut it out," I said, yanking my arm away. "Mom!"

Mom picked out the part she wanted and knelt by the stove. "You can hardly blame him, honey. None of us has ever associated with a stage star before."

"Well," mused Isadora, "there was that good-looking young man I met in Hollywood years ago,

99

but I believe he was in film."

"Were you scared, Vickie?" Matthew asked, his eyes big.

"Only at first, because I met Peter and he said—"

"Stop keeping us in suspense!" Mom said impatiently. "What part do you play?"

"Well, actually . . . construction crew member."

Isadora gave me a puzzled frown. "I don't recall any construction crew in *Romeo and Juliet*. Is this some sort of newfangled modern adaptation?"

I had to admit it sooner or later. I took a deep breath and said, "The truth is, I chickened out. Instead of auditioning, I signed up to be on the construction crew."

There was a dramatic silence, while I waited for them to moan and be disappointed and all. But when I finally got the courage to look them in the eye, they only looked a little surprised.

"What a wonderful opportunity," said Isadora. "One more artist in the family."

Mom went back to peering inside the stove. "I told you there were good jobs off the stage, didn't I? In a way, you're following in the footsteps of your mother."

"Except I don't intend to swing from any rafters."

Isadora had been right about the stove. It didn't take long to get it back together. In no time, she was standing at a burner, stirring something delicious. Her floppy sleeves were tied down with rubber bands, and she had a bandanna over her hair. The soup bubbled and smelled delicious.

*I'm beginning to like old Isadora,* I thought, as I put soup bowls around the table. Dad says you can win over your worst enemy by making them dinner, and I think he's right.

I babbled during the whole meal, all about the show. There were a whole mess of kids on the construction crew.

"There's just one problem," I said between hot spoonfuls of soup. "Mr. Snow says he needs a good set designer."

Isadora put down her spoon abruptly. "Set designer?" she asked, her voice getting squeaky. "He needs a set designer?"

"Yeah. The last one built windmills that fell on the actors' heads."

Matthew slapped the table. "I forgot about that!"

"Anyway," I said, "he doesn't want the art department to do it again. He wants someone artistic."

Suddenly Isadora jumped out of her chair and hurtled across the room to her yellow bag. We all stared at her, spoons still in our hands. *Oh, boy,* I thought. *She's finally lost it. She's cracked up.*

"Mother," said my mom, calmly. "What exactly are you doing?"

"I know there's a pencil in here, somewhere, I just know it," she was muttering. She held up a tiny yellow stub. "Aha! There you are. Now, there must

101

be paper, too, just a little piece. Okay, now, Victoria. Whom do I see? Mr. Blizzard?"

The awful truth began to creep in. Isadora wanted to go to my school and be part of my play. *This is the last straw*, I thought. *I might as well die of embarrassment right here.*

"The job will take a lot of time," I said, feebly.

"Never mind, never mind. I have plenty of time. No one around here needs me much, anyway."

Mom gave her a look that would wither grapes to raisins. "*Mother—*" she said.

Isadora pointed the pencil lead at the paper. "Come on, come on. What's the name?"

*Whenever things start going well,* I thought, *something awful happens.* Now my crazy grandmother was coming to school.

Isadora was still waiting, giving me one of her sharp-old-bird looks.

"Mr. Snow," I said, slowly. "That's S-N-O-W."

# 18

"Watch it, Vic. You almost hammered your hand that time."

She was supposed to be memorizing her lines, but Chels was bugging me up on stage instead. She leaned heavily over my shoulder. "Except for your aim," she added, "you're doing pretty well."

I sat down on the dusty stage floor. "Don't be so shocked, okay? I'm not a total klutz, you know. Talent is supposed to run in the Shippley line." I squinted at my work. "Not bad. Not bad at all."

"Can't you just picture your best friend standing against it in her Shakespearean costume?" She struck a dramatic pose.

"Yeah, and saying her one whole line."

She scowled. "More than one line, my dear. Lady Montague is an important character."

"—who doesn't talk much."

Her face brightened into the old metal Bixler grin. "Can't be the star every time," she said, sitting down cross-legged beside me.

I feathered out the edges of a cloud. I was getting good at this. "Looks like this might be a good show after all," I said.

"—many thanks to your grandma. We've never had such good scenery. She's really talented."

We both glanced over at her. She was standing on the edge of the stage, talking to Mr. Snow and using a wet paintbrush to make a point. She was practically shaking it in his face. In her jeans and a big old sweat shirt, she looked pretty low key, even if she didn't look like your typical grandmother. All of a sudden, her head went back and she laughed. Her voice echoed in the dark auditorium.

Chels made a low whistle. "What's *wrong* with her, anyway? She's acting so normal."

"Maybe it's a phase," I said, slapping dust off my jeans. "She'll probably snap out of it soon."

"I don't know," said Chels, shaking her head. "I think she's getting worse. Yesterday she brought cookies to rehearsal. They were like cookies any grandma would make. They were good."

She was right. Making cookies was a sure symptom of becoming a real grandmother.

"I wouldn't mind if she toned down a little," I

said, "at least while she's working on the play."

"I think she's great just the way she is," said Chels. "Besides, if she got too normal, she'd probably give up set design and painting. Then where would Keats be?"

"But if she wasn't so eccentric, our courtship plan might have worked," I reminded her. "That was a bomb, and it was all because she's not normal."

Chels got her Mysterious Look. It's a look I've seen her use on Grant Hirshfield.

"Don't be so sure."

"What do you mean?"

"*I* think he's interested."

"I bet Mr. Wilkes didn't say that!"

"He didn't have to. I could just tell."

"Intuition?"

"Right."

A voice rang out from the darkness. "Hey, you two!"

It was Isadora.

"What's all the chatter about?" she shouted over. "This scenery won't get built on its own. Just because you're my granddaughter, Victoria Hope Mahoney, don't think you can get away with slacking off!"

Argh. Now the whole world knew it. I gave a good hard whap to the scenery with my hammer.

"I think she's snapping out of it," Chels muttered, rolling her script and standing up to get back to rehearsing.

I didn't mind working alone. I dipped a brush into bright blue and went to work on the sky. It was quiet in there, very quiet. Even Isadora was quiet, going from person to person, checking the work.

Then the door opened in the back of the auditorium. A bright slice of light cut through the dingy room.

"Who's there?" Isadora called out in a gruff voice.

"Hi!" came back a cheerful, familiar voice. "It's me—Harold Wilkes."

"Oh," she said, her voice softening. "Harold, come on in. I want you to see what I've been working on."

Sitting in the front row memorizing lines, Chelsie telegraphed me a sly look. "See?" it said. "I was right. You can trust my intuition every time."

# 19

Sometimes I feel guilty for getting over it. I mean, it's not as though I don't think about Jessica sometimes. I do. It's strange to think that I could have had a baby sister by now. She would have cried a lot, I guess. Laughed, too, at Matthew's funny faces. (He does some great faces. Even I laugh at them.) She would have slept in the old crib. Sometimes when you think of stuff like that, you feel funny.

But I've been really happy a couple of times since Jessica died. At school things are pretty much the same as always. I still eat lunch with the same people, and we still laugh at dumb things. We laugh until we're practically sick.

I get the feeling that my parents will never get over it. I mean, my mom has this look; it's hard to explain. She'll be laughing and all of a sudden it's like she's gotten the flu or something. And then she's not quite laughing anymore.

And you've got to know my dad to understand how he's changed. He's quieter, and *that's* really something. Dad is not a quiet person. He used to make me mad because he was always cracking jokes when you wanted to be serious. But sometimes now I wish he were still like that. He just sits. I've seen him stare at one page in a book for half an hour. I wonder what he's thinking about.

Things are just different.

Mom said once that our family knows what it's like to be really sad, sad down to its bones. I don't necessarily think that's a good thing.

Last week some lady we know came up to Dad and me in the grocery store. The two of them talked boring adult stuff, and I started comparing the food in her cart and ours. You can tell a lot about people by their groceries. Ours, I noticed, had its share of vegetables and stuff that's good for you. There was bubble bath for Matthew. And vitamins.

Her cart was stocked with junk—supersweet cereals, cookies, punch drink. There was also a jumbo size box of laundry detergent beneath. Her kids probably had lots of cavities, but always wore clean clothes.

Next I added up the price of our groceries in my head. My guess was $58.25. I was just starting to add tax when Mrs. Nordquist said something that made me lose track.

"Well, at least the baby wasn't born alive; you can be thankful for that. Imagine if it had been born alive and *then* died. That would have been really terrible."

Dad didn't say much. He just let her talk, but he had this kind of hurt look on his face.

I was so angry, I was shaking. I didn't even say good-bye. I wanted to shout at her. I wanted to yell. My voice would echo up and down the aisles: "How would you have liked it, Mrs. Nordquist?"

We bagged our own groceries ($67.87), loaded up the car, and drove home. Neither of us mentioned what had happened.

Isadora came to watch us—Matthew, mostly—while my parents went to their appointment. They were going to see a counselor to talk about how sad they were about Jessica.

"We won't be long." Mom buttoned her raincoat and felt for the car keys. "We only get fifty minutes a session." She smelled as if she were going to a party, but her face looked tired.

Dad gave her arm a squeeze. "Better go or we'll be late."

I watched them from the big window, feeling a little depressed. You don't expect a counselor to get counseling, that's all. You don't expect your parents to, either.

Isadora's voice woke me out of my thoughts. She was calling from somewhere far away, and I tilted my head to listen.

She wasn't on the second floor. I checked all the bedrooms. I climbed up the flight of stairs to my room, too. No Isadora. Then I noticed that the door to the storage space was open. I squatted down and took a look.

She and Matthew were in there, all right. They were sitting on a dirty old box with newspapers and stuff all around them.

"There you are, Victoria," Isadora said, motioning me in. "You're missing something important."

Yuck. I inched in slowly, because there are mice in the storage space. It's like an attic in there, with a low slanted ceiling and dust and boxes everywhere.

"This place gives me the creeps," I said.

"Don't be silly," said Isadora, waving her arm impatiently. "This is nothing. I could tell you stories— But you'd never believe them, anyway. Not without my slides to prove them."

I bumped Matthew over so I could sit on the edge of the box. "No one ever comes up here," I said, practically sliding off. I gave him another bump.

"Why not?" Isadora roared suddenly. "Get in touch with your environment! Get in touch with your roots!" She waved her arms, and the bright jade-colored kimono gave her wings. "This place is absolutely dense with history," she went on, really getting into it. "Can't you feel it?"

She stopped and looked at us critically. We were sitting there like two lumps. I think Matthew's mouth was open a little.

"You're skeptics. I can see I'll have to show you. Here. Look at this. This is a photo album I gave your parents at their wedding."

She whapped the album open on her knees and flipped a page. There was this picture of a little girl with a frilly dress and funny knobby legs. Stiff petticoats made the dress stand out like a tutu. There was a straw hat on her head, with a too-tight elastic under her chin.

Matthew went beserk. He almost fell off the box, laughing. I have to admit it was pretty funny.

"That's your mother. She was about three in this picture. Look at those curls. Peculiar child. Ate peas one at a time, after she'd lined them up in a row on her plate."

There were plenty of Christmas shots. A tall man with loads of slicked-back hair was in some of them. And beside him, with long slender arms and a complicated hairdo, stood an elegant woman in a wide skirt and matching sweater.

"In my younger days I was more traditional, but I got over it," Isadora told us, briskly turning the page. In the next set of Christmas pictures the tall

111

man was missing. Isadora had her arm around Mom's shoulder, and they were both kneeling by a huge decorated tree. They didn't look very happy.

"Now we hit the teenage years," she said, turning over a loose page. "There she is. Roberta Shippley, age fourteen."

Mom's hair was in a bubble hairdo, with little points of hair plastered to her cheeks. She had on gobs of makeup.

"Eighteen," said Isadora, flipping a page.

It was Mom all right. Her long hair needed a trim. There was an Indian headband around her forehead. She looked sort of like a nerd.

"Wait till you see this picture of my future son-in-law. This is how he looked when I first met him." Her thin finger pointed to a shot of a shortish guy with wavy wild hair and kind of a sad and scrawny moustache. He was grimacing into the camera.

I put my head in my hands. "To think I had such strange parents," I groaned. "I just hope no one ever finds out."

"Victoria, I'm ashamed of you. Strangeness makes the world interesting. Everyone's odd, one way or another. Frankly, I enjoy being a little strange."

Not me. I had my future to consider.

Then Isadora wanted to see pictures of Matthew and me when we were little kids. I ran downstairs and got our family albums. There were a lot of

112

really dumb-looking school portraits of me.

When Mom and Dad got home we had to explain how come we were all covered with dust.

"This baby-sitting stuff is fun," Isadora told them, picking a cobweb off her kimono. "I could be persuaded to do this more often."

# 20

I invited Peggy Hiltshire to the dress rehearsal for *Romeo and Juliet*. "It's free," I told her, "on account of I'm on the stage crew. You can be my guest." My whole family was coming the following night, and I wanted to know what to expect.

"I'd love to go," said Peggy, as if I had asked her for a date.

"Meet me outside your last class."

We didn't get to the auditorium till late, because Peg said first we had to go down to the wrestling room. I don't think she's interested in wrestling at all. I think she's interested in wrestlers. After a while I told her we had to go. The smell was getting to me.

The auditorium door squeaked when we sneaked

in. Chelsie was just about to say her biggest line. She did okay.

The thing that hit me between the eyes was how professional the scenery looked. And I had helped create it. My heart did a little jig. I decided not to point out to Peg how good it was, even though she doesn't notice things unless you practically put them in her face.

The play itself was good, too. The guy playing Romeo had this wild English accent. Juliet was a ninth grader, and she kept making herself cry. I could never do that. If I'm not sad, forget it. I guess if that was what it took to be a good actor, I'd have to stick to set construction after all.

Peggy thought the play was romantic.

"I just love love, don't you?" she whispered.

She really said that, no lie.

During the show, Mr. Snow was calmer than normal. Occasionally he would stop the actors and say something like, "I'd like you to move stage left after that line, please," very calmly, or, "Give me more passion!" It was amazing.

Afterward, I clapped loudly to make up for there not being very many people around. Peggy did, too.

"Well?" demanded someone behind us. "What did you think?"

I gave myself whiplash turning around. It was Isadora. She'd been sitting behind us all the time.

"It was good," we both said together.

"Isadora," I said, "this is my friend Peggy

Hiltshire. Peg, this is Isadora Shippley. Isadora designed all the sets."

"Really?" squealed Peggy. "Ma'am, I just have to say congratulations. The scenery was terrific."

Brother. When she turns on the charm, she goes all out.

Suddenly there was the clatter of feet on stage, and the squeak of wheels. Romeo was pushing out a cart. There was a cake with candles on it, and the whole cast was following—leotards and all. Everyone started singing, "For They Are Jolly Good Fellows." Then they all clapped and yelled for Mr. Snow and Isadora.

First they made Mr. Snow make a speech. He said he was sorry for yelling at everyone so much. And of course he thought we had a great show.

Then Isadora was supposed to speak. She stood by a microphone and got all choked up. "Thanks, everyone," she said in a watery voice. "You've all been so professional; it's been a thrill. And I want to thank my granddaughter, Victoria Mahoney, for helping me get this job in the first place."

We all stood around and ate cake (except Peggy, who said she was on a diet). Some pretty strange guys on the crew tried to get me with tempera paint, but I was too quick for them. Everyone was feeling good.

"I didn't know Isadora was your grandmother," Peter said, coming up to me. "She's the greatest. I wish I had a grandmother just like her."

116

# 21

I love May. It's muddy and breezy, and you never know which coat to put on, your winter one or your spring windbreaker. And every year there's at least one crazy bird outside my window who starts squawking at about five o'clock in the morning. Winter is quiet and sparkling white, but spring is full of wonderful noises.

It was the morning of the opening performance. Chels and I planned to make the rounds and see if we could interest people in last-minute ticket purchases. I stretched in bed, a tickle of excitement in my stomach. The sun turned my curtains bright colors, and I felt good. Then I smelled a delicious smell. I sniffed, trying to figure out the mystery.

117

Cake? No, not in the morning. Eggs? No, more exotic than that. Puff Pancakes!

My dad has this recipe for a great breakfast meal. You take a cup of flour and dump in a cup of milk and four eggs and beat it all. Next you melt a third cup of margarine in an iron skillet in the oven. Then you pour the batter into the skillet and pop it back in the oven at 425 degrees. It puffs up, and in twenty minutes you have a Puff Pancake. You cut it into pieces just like a cake and dribble melted butter on it and maple syrup, or maybe some powdered sugar. It's out of this world. That heavenly smell is what I smelled that morning when I woke up, and I knew it would be a good day. Puff Pancakes are a meal for good days only. I pulled on my jeans and a T-shirt.

Matthew was already downstairs. He was still rubbing one eye like he was half asleep, but he knew something was up, too. Puff Pancakes are a sure sign.

"How come we're having pancakes for breakfast?" he was asking my dad, who was patiently stirring orange juice at the sink, bellowing "Ah, Sweet Mystery of Life."

"Because your mother is back on the job at Willowood Retirement Home today. She's just going in to sort through the paper work, but I thought she deserved a royal send-off. Maybe she even deserves a cheer. Hip-hip-hooray—!"

Even though I usually don't talk much in the

118

morning, let alone yell, I joined them in a very loud cheer.

"Pull up a chair," Dad said to us, pointing. "Your celebrational breakfast is almost ready. Would you like one piece of bacon or two?"

It really was like a party. When Mom came downstairs she had on a new lilac-colored skirt and a short-sleeved sweater. She looked fresh, even happy. Dad said she looked ravishing.

"Don't forget," I told her, "tonight's opening night of *Romeo and Juliet*. I have free tickets for everyone."

"I'll only go if I get to sit right up front," said Matthew, his mouth full. "And I get the aisle seat. In case I have to go to the bathroom."

"Okay," I said, rolling my eyes to the ceiling.

"And it better not be boring."

"Look. I saw it and I liked it. It's not boring."

He chewed awhile longer. "Can I bring my girl friend?"

I thumped down my milk glass. "Absolutely not! Dad, tell him—"

Dad got us laughing again. We spent so much time drinking coffee that I had to run to get ready. But I was waiting by the door and humming "Ah! Sweet Mystery of Life" when Chelsie finally rang the bell.

119

# 22

If Shakespeare were alive, he would love opening nights. I do.

There is only one thing that would make opening night better, and that's if they sold popcorn and candy in the lobby. That would add zip to most plays. If things got boring in the second act, you could open the jawbreakers. I bet play attendance would skyrocket.

There were only a few empty seats in the auditorium, but we found a row that had one for each of us, right up front. Matthew, of course, wanted to sit on the end, and Mom and Dad said okay. They didn't know he wanted to read comics by the aisle light.

Mom looked great. She had lost lots of weight. Dad had on his suit coat, and he looked elegant. He leaned over and pointed at my name in the program. "All hail the star."

The kid behind me was a whiner, but I didn't even care. I was too eager for the play to begin.

Peggy Hiltshire walked by with a bunch of her friends. I waved at her and she waved back. Some of the others did, too. I didn't care that I was with my family—at least not much. Maybe they were a little unusual, but they were okay.

I kept looking at my watch. At the last minute, Isadora made her grand entrance.

She came up the aisle from the stage, her hair swept back dramatically. She must have sprayed on tons of hair spray. Her dress was black, very exotic. People were looking. When she crowded in next to us, she smelled good, too. Mr. Wilkes stood up for her.

"Always dress for the occasion," she announced to me, in too loud a voice. "Sorry I'm late. Last-minute emergency backstage. We got it straightened out."

Suddenly the lights went low, and the audience quieted. There was a pause. The curtains started to part, stopped, jerked again and were finally pulled open. Another pause, and then everyone said "Ah."

There were walls and turrets and plants and windows and stairs and a blue sky. It was like being in Verona, where the play takes place. It was the best scenery Keats Junior High School had ever had for a play. Better than *Oklahoma!*, for sure.

The audience broke into applause. The actors, who had just filed on, stopped, looking confused. The applause got louder, and Isadora smiled and smiled. A couple of people turned toward her and held their hands out and clapped. She wasn't a bit embarrassed. I was, a little. When the applause trickled down to a few last claps, the actors began:

*Two households, both alike in dignity,*
*In fair Verona, where we lay our scene,*
*From ancient grudge break to new mutiny,*
*Where civil blood makes civil hands unclean.*

The play had begun.

# 23

Chels wore her stage makeup over to Isadora's apartment. She had a hundred stories, and she was telling them all.

"—The best part," she was saying, "was when Mr. Snow made the stage crew take a bow. I could have died. Did you see Vic's face? You looked embarrassed, Vic."

"I'm a behind-the-scenes type." I knew I was blushing again, even now, after it was all over. "Being on stage makes me nervous."

Isadora passed cookies in fancy paper cups. Very elegant. I picked out three. We all drank hot coffee with our pinkies sticking out—everyone except my mother, who thinks caffeine is for the birds.

When conversation got a little weak, Mr. Wilkes said, "Izzy has presentations to make. Don't you, Izzy?"

*Izzy?*

While old Izzy went off to the bedroom to look for something, Chels passed me a note. "It worked," she had written on the bottom of one of the cookie papers. She was right. When someone starts calling someone else Izzy, wedding bells are just a matter of time.

Suddenly there was a terrific clatter from the bedroom; then Isadora came out with an armload of things.

First, she produced a full-color photograph of Chelsie during one of the dress rehearsals, stage makeup and all, looking pretty professional. Then Isadora handed a wrapped package to my mother.

"What's this?" Mom shook it and held it to her ear.

"It's nothing, just a token. You don't have to open it here."

But Mom was already tearing the paper. Mom has a thing about packages.

It was obviously a painting. Mom held it out in front of her and got a better look, and the room was silent. "Oh, wow," she said.

"I've been working on it since I arrived," rambled Isadora, nervously. "I didn't know if you'd like it or not, but—"

"Mom," she said, "this is Jessica."

We all stared at her. Slowly she turned the gift around. It was the painting of the red-haired girl. To me it didn't look like the pictures of Jessica I had seen. But Dad got up close, and he said, "It *is*."

Mom looked as if she might cry. Or hug Isadora. Or both. She didn't, but it looked like she might.

"We really appreciate this, Mom," she said.

It had gotten too serious, and Mr. and Mrs. Bixler looked kind of uncomfortable. So Mr. Wilkes jumped up and poured everyone a refill of coffee, and Chels told another story—the one about Romeo getting his tunic tucked into his tights.

The whole room broke up with laughter. *Rocked* with laughter. The walls could hardly contain it all. Mrs. Bixler put her hand over her mouth. Mr. Bixler shook. Matthew practically rolled on the floor. And when I looked over at Mom and Dad, they were both laughing hard. They weren't holding back at all.

# 24

Without clearing it with me, Mom was sending copies of the *Romeo and Juliet* program to all of our relatives. On each one, she underlined my name and drew stars by it. It was embarrassing, but kind of nice, too.

"I'm not going to give up writing," I told her, licking and sealing the envelopes she handed me, "but I wouldn't mind working on another play sometime."

"I have to hand it to you, Vickie. You tried something new, you worked hard, and you were a success. That's a real accomplishment." Suddenly she came over and gave me one of her famous hugs.

"What was that for?" I asked.

"I don't know. I just like you." She went back to her seat.

"Mom?"

"Hmm?"

"Do you think you'll ever want to have another kid? You know. A baby?"

She gave me an odd, quizzical look. "No," she said. "I couldn't go through it. It'd be nine months of worry, and the same thing could happen all over again. No way."

I didn't blame her. I knew I could never do it. I'd be too scared.

The room was quiet again, with just the scratch-scratch of pen on envelope. Then she stopped, mid-address.

"But, then again, who knows? I suppose I could change my mind. Maybe, if God gave me the strength, I could do it. Sometimes we have no idea what we can do—with a little help from him."

That made sense. It was like me and the play. Maybe, with God's help, I'd even *act* in a Keats play someday.

"I'll go mail these," I said, gathering the envelopes into a thick handful. Then I gave her my most charming smile. "No telling how much you can accomplish with a little help from your lovable daughter, right?"

# JUST VICTORIA

# I am absolutely *dreading* junior high.

Vic and her best friend, Chelsie, have heard enough gory details about seventh grade to ruin their entire summer vacation. And as if school weren't a big enough worry, Vic suddenly finds problems at every turn:

- Chelsie starts hanging around Peggy Hiltshire, queen of all the right cliques, who thinks life revolves around the cheerleading squad.
- Vic's mom gets a "fulfilling" new job—with significantly less pay—at a nursing home.
- Grandma Warden is looking tired and pale—and won't see a doctor.

But Victoria Hope Mahoney has a habit of underestimating her own potential. The summer brings a lot of change, but Vic is equal to it as she learns more about her faith, friendship, and growing up.

### *Don't miss any books in*
### *The Victoria Mahoney Series!*

#1 Just Victoria      #3 Take a Bow, Victoria
#2 More Victoria      #4 Only Kidding, Victoria

SHELLY NIELSEN lives in Minneapolis, Minnesota, with her husband and two Yorkshire terriers.

# MORE VICTORIA

# Suddenly, life is nothing but problems.

Vic can see that there will be nothing dull about seventh grade . . . if she can only survive it.

First, there are the anonymous notes saying Corey Talbott, the rowdiest and most popular guy in the seventh grade, has a crush on *her*. It's ridiculous, of course. But who could be writing them? And what will Vic do if Corey finds out?

Then, thanks again to the mysterious note sender, Victoria gets sent to the principal's office—the first time in her life she's faced such humiliation. What will her parents say? The last thing they need is one more thing to argue about. . . .

Live the ups and downs of Vic's first months of junior high in *More Victoria*.

### *Don't miss any books in The Victoria Mahoney Series!*

SHELLY NIELSEN lives in Minneapolis, Minnesota, with her husband and two Yorkshire terriers.

# ONLY KIDDING, VICTORIA

# You've got to be kidding!

Spend the summer at a resort lodge in Minnesota . . . with her *family?* When she's been looking forward to endless days of good times with her new friends from school?

Victoria can't believe her parents are serious, but nothing she can do or say will change their minds. It's off to Little Raccoon Lake, a nowhere place where she's sure there will be nothing to do.

But the summer holds a lot of surprises—like Nina, one year older and a whole lot tougher, who scoffs at rules . . . and at Vic for bothering to keep them. And the bittersweet pang that comes with each letter from her best friend, Chelsie, reminding Vic of what she's missing back home. But the biggest surprise is Victoria's discovery of some things that have been right under her nose all along. . . .

*Don't miss any books in*
*The Victoria Mahoney Series!*

#1 Just Victoria        #3 Take a Bow, Victoria
#2 More Victoria        #4 Only Kidding, Victoria

SHELLY NIELSEN lives in Minneapolis, Minnesota, with her husband and two Yorkshire terriers.